Half My Life

Melissa Novak

© 2015 Melissa Novak

All Rights Reserved.

No part of this publication may be reproduced, stored in a retrieval system, or transmitted, in any form or by any means, electronic, mechanical, photocopying, recording, or otherwise, without the written permission of the author.

First published by Dog Ear Publishing
4011 Vincennes Rd
Indianapolis, IN 46268
www.dogearpublishing.net

ISBN: 978-1-4575-3761-5

This book is printed on acid-free paper.

This book is a work of fiction. Places, events, and situations in this book are purely fictional and any resemblance to actual persons, living or dead, is coincidental.

Printed in the United States of America

To my husband and my parents-
Thank you for always believing in me.

Chapter 1

As I stare out the window of the waiting room, I fold my arms across my chest and sigh in frustration. From the fourth floor, I can see people walking from the hospital building to their cars. A couple of girls have been chatting and laughing the entire way to their car. I envy their carefree spirit, and get lost in thought of what it'd be like to have no worries.

"Abrielle," Grandma says gently, snapping me out of my daydreams. "It's going to be okay. I'm going to fight this as best I can." She smiles, and I can see the positivity in her eyes.

I walk toward her and wrap her in my arms. "I know, but it's not fair," I say as I fight back tears.

"I watched you battle cancer almost three years ago, and your mother battled for a long time, too," she says.

I pull back and search her deep brown eyes. "The strength of both of you gives me hope," she says with a smile so sincere that I believe her.

"You know I'll help you in any way I can." I squeeze her hand and look at the time on my cell phone. We have been waiting for the oncologist to come back with treatment options for at least half an hour. I tap my foot impatiently, and my grandma sits down. She has a sense of peace about her, which is strange for someone who was just diagnosed with stage III lung cancer.

Someone knocks on the door, but doesn't wait for an answer. Dr. Claussen walks in with his resident, a nurse, and an overflowing file. "Faustina," he says as he sits down. "I am confident that you will do well in this battle with lung cancer. Of course there will be some side effects. You'll lose your hair, experience fatigue…" He continues to rattle off side effects, but I'm lost in the monotony of his voice. He uses no inflection as he speaks, almost like he is bored. His message sounds rehearsed, like he has delivered this speech hundreds of times. *He probably has*, I think to myself. I notice he doesn't say that Grandma has a good chance, or that she will definitely beat it, but only that she will do well in the battle, whatever that means. I try not to cry.

The nurse is setting papers in front of my grandma, and pointing to descriptions of different side effects as the doctor addresses them. I look at the doctor's resident. She doesn't look much older than me. Her light brown hair is pulled back into a neat bun at the nape of her neck. She's listening attentively, which boggles my mind, because this doctor's voice is so dull. He's still listing the possible side effects, which I know all too well. I try not to remember what it was like to deal with them. I close my eyes and make an effort to clear my mind, but instead I notice how parched I am, and I'm instantly reminded of the dry mouth I experienced when I endured chemotherapy. I open my eyes and notice Grandma is listening with a polite smile on her face.

She must sense my unease about all of this, because her hand finds mine, and I am instantly filled with peace. I should be the one comforting her, not the other way around.

* * * * *

As we walk to the car, I link arms with her. She is two inches taller than me, standing at six feet, which is pretty tall for someone in her late sixties. Her shoulders do not hunch like most women her age. Her height gives her the appearance of a strong woman, and she walks with confidence. She always has. "So, what are your thoughts?" I ask as we approach her car. I had offered to drive, but she wouldn't let me. She said that my accompanying her to the oncologist's office was enough to ease her nerves. She's stubborn that way.

"I know the road ahead of me isn't going to be easy," she says as we get into the car. "I will need your help at times, but I'm going to get through this."

I nod in agreement. We climb into the car and sit in silence for a moment. I'm not sure what to say. Do I try to comfort her? Should I be real with her about how horrible chemo is going to be? Share what I went through on my own journey?

Finally she breaks the silence. "How do *you* feel about all of this?" she asks.

I wasn't expecting that question. I want to tell her that I'm scared for her. It's one thing to have cancer yourself, and believe you can fight it because you set your mind to it. It's another thing to believe that someone you love can fight it, because you never really know for sure what's going on in their mind. They might say they are going to fight hard, but then have doubts in their mind and never tell you about them.

"It's upsetting that you have to go through this." I pause, because I don't want to sound cliché, but what I'm about to say is true. "As much as it sucks cancer made me a stronger person, and I know you'll be stronger because of it, too." I smile sympathetically.

"You always try to find the positive in a situation, Abrielle. Your mother was like that, too."

I wish my mom had been there for me when I battled cancer. Whenever my side effects were in full swing, I always wondered if she had experienced the same thing—or something worse. I can't believe I have to watch someone I love battle cancer again.

The twenty-minute drive back to Grandma's house seems like five minutes, as we talk the rest of the way about dealing with the side effects of chemotherapy. I make a list of some over-the-counter drugs and other things that might be helpful to her while we talk. When we pull into the driveway, I offer to go get the items on the list, but she smiles and says, "Abrielle, I still have a few days before treatment begins. I will be fine. I have the energy and time to do it myself right now, but thank you for offering." She coughs, and I have trouble believing she can prepare for chemo herself. "Plus," she adds as she points two houses down, "I'm sure Jace would be happy to help me if I need it." She coughs again.

As she says Jace's name, he looks over at us, and takes one hand off the lawn mower handle to wave, as if he knows she is talking about him. I smile and wave back, trying not to stare. *When did he get so cute?* I ask myself, trying to recall what he looked like the last time I saw him. It had been about two months since he came to visit the homeless shelter in Washington, D.C. His mother founded both locations, and he manages the North Beach location, but he often comes to D.C. to check in.

I get out of the car and start to walk toward the front door. "You don't need to walk me in. I know you're busy," Grandma says. "You were at the oncologist's office all day with me. Go home. I'm sure your dad and Ariana are waiting for you to fill them in on today's adventure."

I look at her quizzically. At first, the word *adventure* seems odd. I wouldn't refer to battling cancer as an adventure. But then I remember that when Ariana and I were younger, every time we went somewhere with our grandma, she called it an "adventure." We had "adventures" at the beach, at the grocery store, even at the library; although you could hardly call checking out some books an adventure, she had a way of making it fun. A huge grin stretches across my face thinking of those times, and I hug her tight. "I love you."

"I love you, too." She winks at me, then walks up her front steps.

I watch her until she goes inside, and stare at the front door. "Please, God, don't take her away from me, too," I whisper.

As I turn to leave, Jace is standing there smiling. I didn't even hear him approach. His white T-shirt, drenched in sweat from the mid-summer heat, clings to his body. His blond hair is wet, as if he just stepped out of the shower. A few pieces stick to his forehead. His blue eyes reflect the bright sunlight. Random grass clippings decorate his legs.

"Hi, Abrielle, how are you?" he asks in his slight British accent.

"I've been better," I reply with a forced smile. I want to scream that I'm not okay; that I wish it was me battling cancer, not her. And that I wouldn't wish chemotherapy upon my worst enemies, because the side effects are tormenting. I don't want her to suffer the way I did. "How are you?" I ask, trying to keep my voice calm despite the angry thoughts running through my head. "I haven't seen you at the D.C. location lately."

"Miss me?" he jokes with an even bigger smile than the one he greeted me with.

I smile back, but before I think of something funny to say, he asks about my grandma.

"How is she? She hasn't been outside as much lately. Usually she waters her flowers, or sits on the porch swing reading. I always see her on my way to work, but the past few weeks, she hasn't been out." He sounds worried.

"Really?" I ask in a voice higher than normal, as I raise my eyebrows. "She didn't mention anything to me about fatigue," I mutter. I remember how tired I was before the doctors discovered I had stage I lymphoma, and know that it's very possible she has been less active due to fatigue. I take a few steps toward him. "Can you do me a favor?" I ask.

"Anything," he offers.

I lower my voice, as if Grandma could hear me from inside the house. "Keep an eye on her. Let me know if she seems any...different." I pause, and he looks concerned. I debate whether or not to tell him. I've known him for a few years, through volunteering and working at the shelter, but we have never been close friends. However, he's never given me a reason not to trust him, and he does help my grandma often with things around the house.

I decide to tell him. I lean in. "We just came back from the oncologist's office. She has stage III lung cancer." His facial expression flashes from concern to disbelief.

"Abrielle, I'm so sorry. Is she going to be okay?" he asks.

I try to fight back tears for the second time today. "I'm not sure," I say quietly. I'm honestly worried that she won't do well because of her age.

"Do you want to hang out later, and we can talk about it?" he asks.

"I can't. I have to work," I reply. "I'll see you around."

"Okay. 'Bye," he says with sadness in his voice. He looks like he wants to say more, but doesn't. He just stands there on her front lawn as I walk to my car.

* * * * *

The drive back home to Georgetown feels like the longest ride of my life. Fifty minutes from North Beach is not too bad of a drive. I know I will hit traffic as I get closer to the city. My mind is racing, trying to think of ways I can help my grandma. I recall what I went through during my own battle, and I wonder if she will experience the same things, or if it will be worse: body aches, nausea, hot flashes, dizzy spells, appetite changes, chills, extreme fatigue, and more. I look at the clock on my dash and realize I'm going to be late for work. I picked up a security shift that starts at 6 p.m. I call Eva, my manager, to let her know I'm running behind.

When I get home, I rush through the front door of our house. Ariana jumps up from the couch, as if she has been sitting there just waiting for me to get home. Her strawberry-blond hair frames her face, stopping just below her chin; making her appear more mature than she actually is. Her blue eyes are wide, and full of questions.

"Bri, did you forget that your cell phone is fully functioning? You could have called me right away with the test results," she says with a snap in her voice that teenagers use so often.

"Where's Dad?" I ask in a hurried voice, ignoring her comment. I need to get ready for work, and I'd prefer to tell them the results together so they can console each other if need be. It's hard to accept the fact that someone you love so much has to go through the suffering of chemotherapy and all the struggles that cancer brings.

"He's working late again," my sister says as she rolls her eyes.

I'm not surprised, I think to myself. Once I was officially in remission, he went back to working long hours. "I'm sure that his law office has a lot on their agenda, but he knew I would be coming home today with the results from his mother's CT scan," I complain. I bet after everything our family has gone through, he just doesn't want to deal with it.

"Welllll, are you going to tell me what happened, or do I need to call Gram and ask her myself?" she exclaims as she folds her arms across her chest. She reminds me of our mom. Her pale skin is covered in freckles. She looks beautiful, even when she's frustrated. I stare at her hair again, and I wonder if I should cut mine as short as hers. Mine comes down a few inches past my shoulders. Our hair color is one of the things we both shared in common with our mom.

"She has stage III lung cancer. A few rounds of chemotherapy, then they reevaluate. Possibly radiation, but right now there are too many tumors. Starts in a few days." I let my words sink in. She doesn't look as frustrated as I felt in the oncologist's office.

"Well, that sucks," she says in a matter-of-fact tone. She's witnessed the effects of chemotherapy up-close twice—with me and with our mom. She plops down on the couch and sighs.

"Are you going to be okay?" I ask gently.

"Yeah. You can go to work." She stares off into space. "I'll tell Dad when he gets home." Her eyes look glossy. I hate to leave her alone after sharing that kind of information, but I'm already running late for work.

As I'm running back out onto the front porch, I hear someone calling my name. I would know that voice anywhere. "Hey, Bri, wait up a minute!" shouts Quin as he dashes down his front steps toward me.

My eyes light up, and even though I'm running late for work as it is, I don't care. I've had a crush on Quin since we were in junior high together, and I don't see him as often as I'd like anymore. Ever since he started dating some girl named Gabi a month ago, he spends all his time with her. We used to hang out a few times a week. We haven't gone running together since he started dating her, either.

He sprints up to me and hugs me. He smells like fresh deodorant and aftershave. I hold on a little longer than I normally do. "I really needed a hug today," I say, trying to keep my voice steady as the events of the day play out in my mind. It's so hard to accept everything that has just happened.

He releases me, and his green eyes grow wide, searching mine. "Is everything okay?" he asks, his hands gently touching my arms.

"No, not really, but I have to go to work. Can we talk about it in the morning?" I don't want to walk away from his lingering touch, but I need to leave for work at the same time.

"Is it that guy from the shelter bothering you again? I'll—" he starts.

"No, it's not work-related," I interrupt with a small smile. "Five-thirty morning run?" I ask. "We can talk about it then."

"Yeah, I'll meet you out front. Oh, by the way, tomorrow night a few of us are going out for dinner. Wanna come?" he asks.

"Yeah, I'm free." I could use a distraction.

"Good. Gabi will be there, and I really want you two to be friends. You're the two most important women in my life, so you'd better get to know her." He lightly punches my arm, then heads back toward his house. *Ugh*, is all I can think to myself as I get into my sister's old Dodge Stratus. If I had known Gabi would be there, I never would have agreed. I don't want to get to know her better; I want to be in her place. I want to be in his arms, as his girlfriend. At the beginning of the summer, Quin had led me to believe that our friendship would turn into something more. His behavior had changed, and we had even started acting like a couple. Although we hadn't kissed, we came close a few times, and then all of a sudden, he just stopped talking to me for a few weeks. I'm still holding on to a thread of hope that we could end up together.

I crank down the windows in Ariana's car. She has no air-conditioning, and it's still hot outside. It has been an unusually hot summer this year. I really hate driving her car, but there's no way I'm driving my Mustang convertible, which I worked so hard to buy, to a shady part of town and parking it in a homeless shelter parking lot. The thought of my sister using my car while I have hers isn't much more comforting than parking it at the shelter, though. She's a reckless driver.

Chapter 2

I arrive at the shelter and park Ariana's car in the tiny lot behind the building. As I walk to the door, I notice a man standing in the corner smoking. His jeans are torn at the knees, and his white shirt is speckled with sawdust. He looks like he has been on a construction site. His skin is reddish orange, from being outside too much. He exhales, and smoke billows out of his mouth. "Hey, Abrielle," he says in a rough voice as he holds a hand up. He looks to be in his mid-thirties. I don't remember his name.

"Hello." I wave back with a smile, wondering how long it's been since he was last at the shelter. I was never good with names.

People come and go here. Some stay for weeks at a time; others enroll in our Striving for Greatness program, in which they are given apartments for low rent, and they learn job skills. Some we see every once in a while in between jobs or housing, while others we see for a few days or weeks, then they never return again.

I reach the back entrance and look at the security camera. The lock clicks to the unlocked position, and I grab the handle to open the door. I walk through the metal detectors that everyone is required to walk through. Sherina is sitting at the check-in desk, located at the entrance of the cafeteria. She is a college student volunteer, working here for the summer. Her dark brown hair is pulled up in a messy bun on top of her head. "Hey, girl."

"Hey, Sherina," I say as I rush past her to clock in.

The cafeteria is filled with people who are just hanging out, escaping the summer's heat, or waiting for 7 p.m. mealtime. The TV is on in the corner blaring some cartoons. A few kids are gathered around it watching intently. The smell of sweaty bodies mixed with "summer breeze" air freshener, which squirts from the dispenser on the wall behind the check-in counter, fills the air. It always tends to smell somewhat like a locker room in the cafeteria during the summer, despite the fact that it is an air-conditioned building. I scan the room and notice several different clusters of people sitting together. A few people sit alone, staring at their hands, humbled to be here, while a few others are people-watching.

I make my way toward the security office, on the other side of the cafeteria, to pick up my badge and gun. I don't really mind working security, although that's not my normal job here at the shelter. I was hired part-time to coordinate volunteers who come to prepare meals, and to plan activities for those at the shelter. Lately, I have been picking up security shifts because we haven't filled the open position yet. I have been working near forty-hour weeks, which is okay with me, because I don't go back to Georgetown University until the fall.

"Hey, Miss. P!" a little voice shouts, and a young boy runs up to me and wraps his arms around my leg in a hug. My last name is Peregrine, but the kids here call me Miss P. I pat his back as he hugs me. "Hi, Owen, how is your day going so far? Have you been spending a lot of time outside?" His face is tanner than usual. He is about seven years old with shaggy brown hair, and he wears a big grin on his face.

"Look what I found in the garbage today!" he exclaims as he reaches into his back pocket. He pulls out a teal-colored iPod with headphones. "It works, but I don't have a charger, so I only listen to a few songs at a time because I want to save the battery," he explains as he holds it out for me to see.

I squat down so I am at his level. "Did you really find this in the garbage?" I ask, thinking that he might have stolen it from someone.

"Yes, I did, on the other side of town," he says proudly, putting it back into his pocket.

"I think I have an extra charger at home I can give you," I say, standing up.

"Thanks, Miss P!" he exclaims and runs away to his find his older brother. I wonder why someone would throw away a perfectly good iPod. Some people are so wasteful.

I turn around, and Silas is standing behind me, blocking my way to the office door. "You're late," he says in a firm voice. He is not my boss, so I don't really care that he is annoyed with me. He likes to try to intimidate people with his broad stature. He looks the part of a security guard. It's as if he stepped out of a professional wrestling ring and threw some *real* clothes on. He hands me his gun, holster, and security lanyard. "I'm late for a meeting," he states and begins to walk away. "I called in," I shout after him, but he continues to walk away. I'm not sure if he hears me or not. I hang the lanyard around my neck.

For anyone who doesn't know my background, it might seem silly that the shelter manager would put me on security detail. I smile at what I must look like to others by my appearance alone: a twenty-year-old girl, with a regular-sized frame, in charge of protecting the shelter? I don't look very intimidating. If they only knew that my dad put me through martial arts classes and taught me how to use a gun, they wouldn't think I was incapable of protecting the shelter, like Silas does. Dad always said it was important for Ariana and me to feel confident in defending ourselves.

I spend the next four hours patrolling the halls and sleeping quarters, checking entrances to make sure they are locked, looking for any suspicious activity or brewing fights, but it turns out to be an uneventful evening.

As I drive home, the warm summer night's breeze makes me feel sleepy. I stick my left arm out the window and wish I was in my convertible. It's the perfect night to cruise. I turn onto our block. It is lined with cookie-cutter houses. Each house is tall and narrow, sitting very closely to each other. The only difference is the color of the brick and the landscaping in each yard. I pull up in front of our house and climb the front steps. I'm surprised when I open the front door and see that Dad has fallen asleep on the couch with the TV on.

I walk across the hardwood floor, trying not to make any noise. His light brown hair is disheveled, and his tie hangs loosely around his neck. I turn the TV off and start to tiptoe toward my bedroom. "Abrielle," he says softly.

"Sorry to wake you. I was trying to be quiet," I say as I turn around.

He looks exhausted as he gets up from the couch. "Your sister filled me in about your grandmother. I'm going to take off work tomorrow, and go over to her house to help her with some things," he says as he walks toward me.

I nod. "I think she would appreciate that," I say. "How are things at work?"

"Busy as usual," he replies as he rubs his forehead.

"Anything I can do to help?" I ask, already knowing the answer.

"I wish." He kisses my forehead. "Sweet dreams."

"Good night, Dad," I say as he walks down the hall to his bedroom.

Today was mentally exhausting. I fall asleep as soon as my head hits the pillow.

Chapter 3

"Today is a good day to do great things," my peppy voice declares repeatedly from my phone. I roll over to turn it off. I'd set my alarm to that recording of myself, in hopes of beginning my day positively. "Today is a good day to do great things," I mutter as I pull a gray racerback tank over my head. The scar from where I had a portable catheter during chemo is visible when I wear tank tops: a two-inch, horizontal line, a couple of inches below my collarbone on my left side. At first, I was very self-conscious when it would peep out from the neckline of a shirt, but now I consider it one of my battle scars. I comb my hair into a ponytail and walk down the stairs to the kitchen.

I love being the only one awake in the morning. The house is so quiet. I chug a premade smoothie, and then begin stretching in the family room. *How can I best help my grandma?* I ask myself as I lean forward to touch the floor between my feet, stretching my hamstrings. If only I lived closer to her, it would be easier to help her. It would be crazy to drive fifty minutes each way on a daily basis. It just wouldn't be efficient. I grab my gray sneakers and slip them on. Suddenly, it comes to me. *I can move in with her! I can transfer to the North Beach Shelter, temporarily, and take care of her when I'm not working!* I can't help but smile to myself. My dad and sister wouldn't worry about her as much if I was there to help her. I feel relieved that this could really work for everyone, and that I could still keep my job. I reach for my cell phone to call Grandma, excited about the possibility, and then I remember the sun hasn't even risen yet. I will call her after work.

I head out the front door, and surprisingly Quin is waiting for me on the sidewalk. His brown hair sticks out a bit from under his backward red, white, and blue D.C. Natives hat, which reminds me that we haven't been to a game yet this summer. "You look peppy this morning," he says.

"Well, I just had a great idea, one that I'm pretty excited about," I say, smiling.

"Oh yeah, what's that?" he asks as we start jogging down the street.

"Bad news first," I say.

"Oh yeah, I almost forgot about how worried you were yesterday. Is it your grandma's CT results?" he asks.

"How did you know she was getting a CT scan?" I ask.

"Your sister told me about it a few weeks ago," he replies. The sky is starting to lighten up a bit.

"She has stage III lung cancer," I say quietly. He doesn't respond right away, so I stare at the streetlight ahead. We are running through a quiet neighborhood. The street is lined with cars. There's not much going on this early in the morning.

I look over, and Quin seems to be in deep thought. I wonder if he is recalling how I was affected by chemo. He came to visit me every day when I wasn't at the hospital. Some days his visits were five minutes; other times he stayed for hours. He was always there for me during my battle.

Finally he says, "Do you realize that between all the years your mom dealt with cancer on and off, your battle, and now your grandma, that you have spent half your life fighting this stupid disease?"

I calculate the time in my head. He's right. "That's kind of depressing. Thanks for pointing it out," I reply sarcastically.

He snickers at me. "Yeah, it sucks. But it's amazing how you have overcome so many obstacles. You're kind of my role model."

I scoff at his comment.

"I'm serious. It's been ten years and counting that you have had to deal with this, and you're still so positive about everything."

I stare into the distance. "Yeah, well, it's not easy. My mom always said that worry is a thief of joy, hope, and peace, so why waste your time with it?"

"It's hard not to worry."

"I know. She's right, though." We continue running, picking up the pace a bit. The sun is peeking out over the horizon, lighting up the blue sky.

"You know I will help in any way I can, right?" he asks.

I nod my head. "The great idea I just had is to move in with her. I should be able to transfer to the North Beach location for work, and the rest of the time I can be there to help," I reply.

Fifteen minutes later, we are jogging down Thirty-seventh Street, in front of Georgetown University. I love this campus. It's set up on a hill above the Potomac River. The buildings that have survived over two hundred years are perfectly designed in Gothic-style architecture. Some of them look like smaller-scale castles; others look like medieval church buildings. As we run past campus and begin to head back toward home, I notice the beads of sweat dripping down my neck. I look over at Quin. Even when he is glowing with sweat, he's attractive. I wipe the sweat from my forehead, remembering that I will be meeting his girlfriend tonight, and wince.

We kissed when I was a sophomore in high school. He was a senior at the time. We tried dating after that, but it just seemed awkward. Our timing always seemed to be off. Either he was dating someone or I was dating someone, or maybe we were just too scared to risk our friendship. But we have been through so much together, and we know each other so well. I can't imagine my life without him in it.

"Earth to Abrielle," his voice interrupts my thoughts.

"What? Oh, sorry, I was lost in thought."

"Yeah, I could tell," he replies with a grin. The aroma of freshly brewed coffee fills the air as we run past my favorite coffee shop.

"When are we going to a game?" I ask as I nod toward his hat.

"Actually, I was thinking next weekend would be perfect to gather a group and go."

"Sounds good to me. Are you getting tired yet? It's been a while since you came running with me. Being a police officer and all, you should be doing your best to stay in shape," I tease.

"Yeah, yeah. I have been working some overnight shifts lately. I'll race you the last block," he shouts, already sprinting toward our houses.

"Cheater!" I yell, chasing after him.

Chapter 4

I walk into the shelter and head toward the office to clock in for my morning shift. "Good morning, Abrielle!" exclaims Eva. Her light brown hair is pulled back into a low ponytail, and her already bronze skin seems darker from the summer sun. I wish my skin would tan in the sun, but it just goes from red back to pale. A gold metallic eye shadow paints her eyelids, causing her brown eyes to pop.

"Good morning," I reply with a smile. "Good morning, Silas," I add as I look at the back of his head. Staying focused on the security cameras, he makes some sort of grunting noise, which barely sounds like a greeting. I roll my eyes.

"Eva, I wanted to talk to you about something today," I begin.

She peers over my shoulder, looks out the one-way mirrored window, and replies, "We can talk in the afternoon. Your breakfast group is already here." I grab my ID lanyard off the hook by the door, then walk out of the office to greet them.

"Hello. You guys must be the color guard team from Liberty Junior High," I say with a warm smile. A few of the students nod their heads. "Thank you for coming. I'm Abrielle, and I will be helping you get set up in the kitchen this morning." Eight junior high students and two adults stand before me. "It's really great that you are doing a service project as a team," I add. "Let's head to the kitchen and we can get started." I walk toward the front of the group to lead them to the kitchen.

"Excuse me. Would you be able to tell us a little bit about the shelter?" a boy with jet-black hair and glasses asks.

"Sure," I reply with a grin. "But it will have to be after breakfast. Mealtime is at eight a.m., so we only have about forty minutes to cook." I am surprised they don't look sleepy. It's the middle of July. Most kids their age would be sleeping in until ten o'clock, but not this group. Here they are, ready to serve. I walk them into the kitchen, and they set down the bags of groceries they brought. I briefly explain how they should set up the serving area, and then point out the cupboard with the pots and pans. "If you have any questions, I'll be right around the corner in the office. Just knock on the door."

As I push open the door from the kitchen to the cafeteria, I notice Jace standing at the security desk, near the entrance. He looks more professional today than the last time I saw him. He's dressed in khakis and a royal blue polo, which brings out his eyes. His hair is combed over and perfectly in place. Part of me is surprised to see him. He looks to be in deep conversation with Sherina, so I walk into the office to check my e-mail.

Eva is on the phone, and Silas is still glued to the security camera footage. I sit down at my desk and open the Internet browser. Just as I am logging in to my e-mail account, the office door opens and Jace walks in. "Good morning, everyone," he says in a cheerful voice, while looking at no one but me. I could listen to his accent all day long. It's not too heavy, but there are certain words he pronounces differently. It's cute. Eva waves because she is still on the phone. "Good morning," I respond.

Silas turns around and gets up from his chair. He smiles at Jace as he walks toward him. I don't ever think I've seen Silas smile before. He and Jace greet each other with what I like to call a "bro hug." It's like a half hug–chest bump–handshake combo. They seem to know each other very well, which strikes me as odd, because Silas rarely talks to any of the shelter employees. "We'll be back in a few minutes," Jace says as he and Silas walk out of the office. I can't help but wonder where they are going. I wonder if Silas is an old family friend of Jace's, or if they just know each other from working at the shelter.

I check my in-box and see a message there from Jace with the subject line "Charity Ball." Curious, I open that message first, ignoring the other twenty. It's a group e-mail to all shelter employees. It reads:

> Hello Everyone,
> I'd like to invite you to be a part of the planning committee for our annual charity ball. This year the ball will take place at the Wyatt Hotel in Washington, D.C., on the first Saturday in October. Planning meetings will take place on Wednesdays, at the D.C. location at 3 p.m. If you wish to be a part of the committee, we will adjust your work schedule accordingly so that you can attend. The first meeting will take place next Wednesday in the family counseling room.
> Have a great day,
> Jace Pierce

I stare at the e-mail for a few moments. I had totally forgotten that the shelter holds a charity ball each year. In the past I have helped collect donations for the silent auction, but I was never part of the committee. The ball is only open to those ages twenty-one and older, and I fall one month short of the age restriction. I wonder if they will still let me attend since I'm an employee. I'd really like to be part of the planning committee and attend the ball. I've seen pictures before, and it looks like a lot of fun. The charity ball is the main fund-raiser that helps to cover operating costs for both shelters.

A knock on the office door interrupts my thoughts about the ball. I get up and open the door. It is the student who had wanted to learn more about the shelter earlier. He has a yellow stain on his shirt that wasn't there earlier. "I think we have everything set up for breakfast now. Would you be able to come check?" he asks.

I nod my head and begin to walk to the kitchen. "What's your name?" I ask.

"Gavyn." He sticks out his hand.

I shake it as we walk. By now the cafeteria is pretty full of people, waiting for the kitchen to open up for breakfast. A few teenagers are playing cards at one of the tables.

We walk into the kitchen, and I go through the line to make sure they have everything out and in place. Trays and utensils are set out. Milk and orange juice have been pre-poured. The coffee is ready, and the food is almost prepared. "In a minute we will open up these service windows." I point to the two large metal doors that are locked shut, and then to the countertop in front of the food. "The children and women will line up first, take a tray, and then go through the line of food, ending at the drinks. If one of you could stand in front of each food item, you can serve the food onto their trays. Since there are only a few food items to serve, the rest of you could stand by the drinks and make sure there is enough for everyone. Remember that a smile and a positive attitude can really make someone's day," I explain.

The students eagerly pick a station and line up. "Who wants to ring the meal bell?" I ask. Immediately every hand goes up. I pick the tallest girl, closest to the bell. Her hair is a bit knotted on one side, as if she forgot to brush it before she left home. I unlock the service windows, and she rings the bell excitedly.

Children line up with their parents, and women without children line up next. The men usually wait until the line dies down a bit before leaving their claimed tables. While it's unfortunate to see so many homeless and unemployed people, I feel lucky to be part of an organization that provides for them on many different levels. As people pass by in the line, I greet them, making small talk with the ones I know. From young children, to young adults, to middle-aged men and women, to an elderly man with a cane, they are all here for a meal. If you saw any of them walking past you on the sidewalk, you might not realize that they are homeless or living in poverty. Poverty doesn't discriminate against race, age, or gender.

"Good morning, Abrielle," the guy I saw smoking outside yesterday cheerfully greets me.

"Good morning. I have a terrible memory when it comes to names. Can you remind me of yours?" I ask.

"Vander." He smiles.

"Well, Vander, I hope you enjoy your breakfast and have a great day."

"Thanks. You, too." His voice is rough.

The line dies down, and the group begins to clean the griddles and pans that they had used to cook with. Once those who want seconds have had their fill, we begin to clean up the rest of the kitchen. I show a few of the girls how to wrap up and label the leftovers, then I pull down the heavy service window doors and lock them in place. Jace walks into the kitchen and grabs an apple. "Hey, how are you doing today?" he asks.

"Pretty good. How about you?"

He shrugs a shoulder, as if to suggest he's okay. "Did you get my e-mail about the charity ball? I'm hoping you'll join the planning committee."

"Yeah, I want to help with it. But I'm not twenty-one yet. Will I still be able to go to the ball?"

"I think we can make an exception for you," he says playfully. "Now get back to work. It looks like your crew is almost done cleaning." He winks and walks back into the cafeteria.

The junior high students have finished and are standing around talking. "Okay," I say in a loud voice. "Gather around and I will tell you a little bit about the shelter." Gavyn rushes to the front of the group. "The shelter was opened five years ago by a woman named Dalilah Pierce. She runs both this shelter and the location in North Beach, with the help of her son. He was just in the kitchen a few minutes ago. Some of you may have noticed him." A few girls in the back giggle and whisper among themselves. "We provide meals for those who are homeless, those who are unemployed, and those who can't afford groceries. There is no limit to the number of meals people can come in for. Everyone is welcome as often as they need help." The students are listening attentively.

I continue, "People are allowed to stay the night, too. There is a men's room and a women's room for sleeping. They sleep on cots or mats, and they are each given a locker to store their belongings. They cannot stay overnight for longer than three weeks unless they enroll in one of our programs. We have a few different programs in place to help people develop job skills, get their GED, or find affordable housing or jobs."

Gavyn raises his hand. "I was really surprised to see kids and a few teenagers here today. How did they end up here?"

I smile gently. "Well, kids end up homeless for different reasons. Sometimes a parent loses their job, and then they can't afford their house anymore. Sometimes their parent has an addiction, and they spend their money on drugs instead of food. Sometimes they have a house, but they can't afford groceries, so they come here for help. Does anyone else have a question?" No one raises their hand.

"Thank you for allowing us to serve here today," says a balding man with glasses.

"Thank *you* for coming! You're welcome back anytime." As I walk them to the exit, I hear the students talking about coming back with their families, and it warms my heart. Out of the corner of my eye, I see Jace walk back into the office. Perfect timing. I can talk to him instead of Eva about transferring locations. It's ultimately his decision anyway.

I say good-bye to the junior high students and make a beeline for the office. The cafeteria has half as many people in it as it did for breakfast. People who have nowhere to go are welcome to hang out in the cafeteria in between mealtimes, but they are not allowed to go back into the sleeping quarters until 9 p.m. I walk along the wall to the office with my head down, not wanting to stop and chat with people along the way.

I'm anxious to find out if I can transfer locations or whether I will have to find another job. I've worked at this shelter since I was sixteen. I really don't want to find a new job near my grandma's place, but it's important to me to be there for her during her treatment, so I will if necessary. I hope it all works out.

I walk into the office to find Eva tapping away on her computer keyboard. Jace is sitting at Silas's workstation, on that computer. Eva looks up. "What was it you wanted to talk to me about?" she asks with kindness in her voice. I sit down at my desk and swivel my chair to face hers. "I was wondering...if I could temporarily transfer to the North Beach location. My grandma lives in North Beach, and we just found out she has lung cancer. I'd really like to move in with her so that I can take care of her and drive her to doctors' appointments. I'm not sure how long I would need to work there, though. It depends on how long it takes for her to recover from treatment."

Jace swivels around in his chair to face me as I speak.

"Oh, Abrielle, I'm so sorry you have to deal with all of that," Eva says with compassion underlying her voice.

"I'm sure we can work something out. Give me a day or so to figure it out," Jace adds .

"Thanks." I swivel back around to check the rest of my e-mails. I don't want to go into any more detail about my grandma right now, because the thought of her battling cancer both angers and frightens me. Plus, I don't want to break down in front of Jace.

I feel Eva's hand on my shoulder. "Let me know if there's anything I can do to help," she says quietly.

"Thank you." I nod my head. She walks out of the office.

I notice a bright yellow sticky note hanging from the bottom of my computer screen. It states that the lunch group will need to use the grill. I get up from my chair. The e-mails can wait; they will still be there when I return. I walk through the cafeteria and outside into the sweltering heat toward the shed. We have a gated outdoor area with a small patch of grass where kids can play. There is a smoking section, and a picnic table, too. You can only enter this section from the cafeteria. I unlock the padlock on the shed, and the doors swing open. There is so much stuff in here—we really need to clean it out one day when it's not as hot. The grill is buried in the back. Most groups that volunteer prefer to cook inside where it's air-conditioned. We rarely use the grill. It will be a nice treat for our clients.

I walk into the shed and begin to drag the grill out, breaking a sweat due to the humidity. It bumps into things on the way—the lawn mower, a volleyball net, some extra cots.

"Abrielle, let me help you with that," I hear Jace say from behind me. I gladly step aside and let him roll the grill out under the carport into the shade.

"Thanks," I say as he runs his arm across his forehead, wiping away sweat.

"Hey, do you have any plans for next weekend?" he asks.

"I'm going to a Natives baseball game on Saturday evening, but that's it. Why, what's up?"

"You *would* like the Natives," he jokes.

"Loyal fan from the day I could hold a baseball," I reply with my hand over my heart.

"I've always liked the Muskateers better. Friday night, I'm taking my dad's plane out. Do you want to go for a ride?"

"Besides running this place, you're a pilot, too? What else do you do in your spare time?" I am impressed.

"I started learning from my dad as soon as I turned fourteen," he replies.

I have never been on a private plane before, only commercial airlines. It seems thrilling. When else would I get the chance to fly like that? "Yeah, I'd love to!" I exclaim.

"Great! If you will already be at your grandma's place, we can drive to the airport together. It's a date."

As he says the word *date*, I feel my smile fade. I'm not sure if I'm comfortable with calling what we're doing a date. Jace is cute, but I don't know if I like him like that. Is it possible that he's interested in me? I bite my lip.

I think he notices my excitement fading, and he quickly stammers, "I-I-I didn't mean *date*. It just came out." He looks nervous, as if I might change my mind about going.

"It's okay. What time should I meet you?" I ask.

"Seven p.m."

"Okay, I'm looking forward to it. I'm going to go find the grilling utensils now," I say, then head toward the cafeteria entrance.

Chapter 5

Later that evening, I stare into my closet for the third time, as if something new will magically appear. I need to find the perfect shirt for tonight's dinner. This is my first time meeting Quin's new girlfriend, and honestly? I want to look prettier than her. It will boost my self-confidence.

"What are you doing?" Ariana asks from my doorway, as she munches on a bag of pretzels.

"Trying to find the perfect top," I respond.

"Why? Where are you going?"

"To some barbecue restaurant with a few friends."

"Will Quin be there?" she asks.

"Yes."

My sister walks over to my closet and pulls out a shimmery, plum-colored tank top. "Wear this. It compliments your hair and your eyes," she says, and then plops down on my bed.

"What are you doing tonight?" I ask as I spray an anti-frizz curling serum in my hair that will help it lay better. There's no point in straightening it with the humidity outside.

"One of my friends is having a pool party."

"Perfect night for that," I respond as I put on some makeup. "I'm going to move in with Grandma during her treatment. I talked to her earlier," I casually state, looking at my sister in the mirror to see her reaction.

"That's a really good idea," she replies. "Maybe I can stay over a few nights now and then. It will be like old times." Up until the past few years, we used to spend a couple of weeks each summer at our grandma's house.

"Sounds good," I say with a smile. "I have to get going. Have fun at your pool party."

* * * * *

As I pull into the parking lot of Billy's BBQ, I see my best friend, Jocelyn, walking up to the entrance. With the overwhelming news about my grandma, I had forgotten to ask Quin who else was coming tonight. Jocelyn and I have been best friends since the fifth grade. Her neon-pink tank top makes her tanned skin glow. I rush out of my car and through the entrance to greet her. "Heeeyyy!" she screams and rushes over to hug me. We throw our arms around each other.

"How was Florida?" I ask. Her bleach-blond hair is clipped back.

"Amazing! As you can see, I caught a lot of sun!" She holds out her arms to show off her tan.

"You look great!" I exclaim. "I loved all the pictures you texted me from the beach."

"We should go there over fall break! So, are you ready to meet Gabi?" she asks. She knows all about my first week of the summer with Quin and how he led me on. I was afraid I was just making things up in my mind, and since I wasn't ready to risk our friendship by pointing out the change in his behavior to him, I never talked to him about it. I talked to Jocelyn instead.

"Yeah," I sigh.

A rush of warm air blows in the restaurant as Natalia and Paolo walk in through the front doors. They are twins from Italy who have lived in D.C. for a few years. Natalia is working toward her law degree at Georgetown, and Paolo works at the police department with Quin. Both could be models, with their olive skin and prominent Italian features. We all greet each other the European way, with kisses on each cheek.

"This is my first time at a barbecue restaurant," Natalia gushes in her thick Italian accent. She looks around, taking in the country-and-western decorations. Her eyes stop on a poster. "Oh, they have line dancing tonight! We must stay and participate!" she exclaims.

Paolo grabs Jocelyn's hand and twirls her. "Sounds like fun," he says.

Another burst of warm air blows in as the front doors open again, but this time it's Quin and Gabi who walk into the restaurant. Jocelyn throws her arm around my shoulder. Gabi is surprisingly petite. Her dark hair is cut short and sleek, but it still looks feminine and cute. Silver hoops dangle from her ears, and her black dress billows in the wind from the doors opening. She wears five-inch heels, which I would consider painful, but she walks gracefully in them, as if she has had a lot of practice. Quin is holding her hand as they approach us. I feel slightly underdressed compared to her, but as I look at what everyone else is wearing, I realize that she is the one who's *over*dressed. Quin is wearing his Natives cap and a three-quarter-sleeve flannel shirt.

"Everyone, this is Gabi," Quin says, beaming.

Natalia steps forward to greet her, kissing each of her cheeks, then Paolo does the same. Jocelyn sticks her hand out.

"And this is Abrielle," Quin says, as I hold my hand out for Gabi to shake.

"Oh, I've heard so much about you," she gushes enthusiastically.

I wonder what Quin could possibly have told her. We have a long history. Why would he talk to her about me? I want to reply that I've heard nothing about her, but I bite my tongue.

"Party of six?" the hostess asks, interrupting us.

"Yes," Jocelyn replies.

"Right this way."

We follow her to a corner booth. The backrest looks like a red-and-white-checkered picnic tablecloth, and there is a silver lantern in the center of the table. Pictures of cowboys and country singers hang on the wall behind the booth. Jocelyn slides in on the right side, followed by Paolo and Natalia. I climb in from the left side, sliding to meet Jocelyn in the center of the seat. Quin follows, and then Gabi. It's a little tight in the booth, and Quin's left leg rests against my right one. He doesn't move it, though, and I wonder if Gabi notices. The hostess hands us menus and walks away.

"Jocelyn, was it as hot in Florida as it is here tonight?" Quin asks.

"It's about the same. Definitely more humid there, though," she replies, then asks, "Gabi, how did you meet Quin?"

Gabi's lips stretch into a smile, flashing her perfectly straight teeth. "Well, I was speeding, and he pulled me over." Her voice annoys me. It's a bit more high-pitched than most girls'.

"I told her I'd let her off with a warning if she agreed to go out on a date with me," Quin interjects with a smirk.

"No, you didn't!" Paolo grins.

"You're right," Gabi says, nodding toward Paolo. "I actually asked *him* out. It's not every day you get pulled over by the *cutest* officer in Washington, D.C." She stares into his eyes, and he leans in to kiss her.

"Ugh," Jocelyn whispers in my ear.

"Hello, my name is Oliver. I will be taking care of you tonight," our server says, diverting my attention. His dull brown hair is cut short and even all the way around his head. "What can I get you to drink?" Everyone orders an alcoholic beverage except Jocelyn and me. We are the only two under twenty-one, so we both order strawberry lemonades, my favorite. The server walks off to get our drinks.

"Abrielle, Quin told me you work at the homeless shelter. I have always wanted to volunteer there." Gabi seems genuinely interested.

I force a smile. "I think that can be arranged."

"What do you do there?" she asks.

"I coordinate the volunteers, find people to prepare meals, and help with different programs," I respond.

"It sounds like you meet a lot of different people. If there are any opportunities to work with children, I'd love to help with that. I'm a nanny."

"That's admirable," I reply. "I don't think I would have the patience to work with young kids every single day."

Jocelyn bumps my leg under the table. I prefer working with the older kids or adults at the shelter. I feel like I can relate to them better.

"What Bri didn't mention is that she also works security at the shelter," Quin adds.

"Oh? What's that like?" Gabi asks.

The server has come back with our drinks, the alcoholic ones in Mason jars. He begins setting them down in front of us. Gabi gets her drink first and takes a sip, staining the rim of the jar with her red lipstick.

"I get to carry a gun and patrol the building, making sure everyone is safe," I respond.

"I was just telling Quin on the way over here that I don't think I could ever fire a gun. It seems scary." She looks over at Quin. His arm is resting on the booth behind her back, and his fingers trace imaginary lines on her shoulder. I try hard not to roll my eyes at her comment. How is he dating this girl?

"Excuse me," Oliver says politely. "Is everyone ready to order?" We all nod and then give our orders, and the server leaves.

"Speaking of guns, I'm going to the shooting range tomorrow afternoon. Do you guys want to come with me?" Paolo asks, glancing back and forth from Quin to me.

"Sure," I reply. "I haven't actually had to fire a gun in a while, so I could use the practice."

"Yeah, count me in, too," Quin says. I notice that Paolo's hand is now resting on Jocelyn's leg. They had gone out on a few dates before her vacation, but she hasn't filled me in on much since she has been out of town.

"Gabi, have you ever been country line dancing before?" Natalia asks, changing the subject.

"Actually, Quin and I have come here a few times, and we learned a little bit. We aren't that great, but it's really fun," she explains.

"I can't wait to learn!" Natalia says excitedly, clapping her hands together.

"*You* have been line dancing?" I ask Quin in disbelief.

"Yeah," he replies. "She really likes country music, and it is pretty fun." Quin usually stood around socializing at dances in high school even though he is pretty coordinated.

"The things we do for women, right?" Paolo says. Quin has a goofy, love-struck grin on his face as he nods. I try to focus my attention on the flame flickering inside the lantern on the table.

"They give everyone who wants it a free twenty-minute lesson before they open up the dance floor. It's nice the way they instruct you, because you don't have to come with a partner," Quin adds. We talk for a few more minutes about country dancing, and then the server brings our meal. Quin orders another drink. The thought hadn't crossed my mind that I wouldn't have a partner until he brought it up. Maybe I can find a cute guy to dance with—and make Quin jealous.

Suddenly I feel my phone vibrating in my purse. I pull it out and see Jace's name on my screen. I only have his number programmed in my phone because he is a manager at the shelter, and I have all the manager's numbers. I wonder why he is calling me on a Friday night. I usually don't answer my phone when I'm out with friends, but I'm concerned it might be about my grandma. "Excuse me, I have to take this call," I say. Quin and Gabi slide out of the booth so that I can get by. I hit the Answer button and put the phone up to my ear. "Hang on a second," I say as I walk to the front doors of the restaurant and step outside, where it's a bit quieter. "Hey, what's up?" I ask.

"Sorry to bother you. It sounds like you are out," he replies.

"Yeah, I'm having dinner with some friends."

"Well, I just thought you would be excited to know that we can transfer you to the North Beach location."

"That's so great!" I exclaim.

"We actually need a part-time security guard there, if that works for you."

"Yeah, I can do that," I respond. I don't mind working security at all. It's actually kind of thrilling. "When I saw your name on my caller ID, I thought maybe something had happened to my grandma," I add.

"Oh, sorry to worry you. I should have texted. I'll check on her tomorrow morning and send you a message."

"Okay, thanks for letting me know about work. I really appreciate the call."

"No problem. I'll see you at the meeting for the charity ball on Wednesday."

"Okay, have a good night," I reply and hit the End Call button.

When I get back to our booth, Quin and Gabi stand up to let me back in. "Is everything okay?" Quin asks, with a hint of worry in his voice.

"Yeah." I slide in the booth.

"Quin told me about your grandmother earlier. I'm really sorry," Gabi says. "If there's anything we can do to help, let me know."

"I can't believe you didn't tell me!" Jocelyn says with a look of concern.

"We just found out, and I didn't want to ruin your vacation with bad news. She'll be okay."

Natalia reaches across the table and grabs my hand. "Our brother back home had leukemia. We know what it's like to witness someone battle cancer."

Jocelyn wraps her arm around my shoulder for a side hug and Quin glances at me knowingly. Only Jocelyn and Quin know about my family history with cancer,

"We're here for you," Natalia adds.

"Thanks. Let's finish up here and hit the dance floor!" I say, changing the subject. I don't want to talk about cancer right now, but it's nice to know that I have support from so many people.

Everyone except Jocelyn and me orders another drink. We pay our bills and head out to the dance floor in the other room, which is separated from the restaurant. The lesson for beginners is just starting. "Welcome to Country Line Dancing 101. I'm Lydia, and I will be your instructor for the evening," a thin woman says in a pleasant voice. Her blond hair is braided into pigtails, and a light brown cowgirl hat sits on her head. She is wearing a ruffled white tank top and cut-off jean shorts. She looks like she just stepped out of a country music video.

"We are going to go over two different group dances tonight. We'll practice first without the music, and then add it in," she says with a smile. Everyone lines up in rows, Jocelyn on my right, with Gabi on my left and Quin next to her. Natalia and Paolo line up behind us.

Lydia goes over a few simple steps, using four counts. We move a few steps to the right, a few to the left, and then kick each leg out in front of us twice, and turn. Finally she adds in the music. "This is easier than I thought," I say to Jocelyn. She nods in agreement. When the song finishes, the instructor teaches a new set of steps to a different dance. Then we practice with the music again. After the lesson, Jocelyn and Paolo stay on the dance floor, while Natalia, Gabi, and I go over to one of the tables that are scattered around the perimeter of the room. Quin walks over to the bar to buy drinks for him and Gabi. If his goal is to get drunk tonight, he's going to attain it soon.

We are barely sitting for one minute when two older gentlemen with gray beards and cowboy hats approach us. "Would any of you ladies care to dance?" asks the one on the right, who is wearing a button-down, checkered shirt. We all look at each other.

"You two go ahead," says Gabi with a smile. Natalia and I walk to the dance floor with the two men.

"I'm Abrielle," I say to the one who takes my right hand in his left. He puts his left arm on my waist, so I put my other arm on his shoulder.

"Pretty name," he replies. "I'm Winston, and that's my friend Cal," he says, nodding toward Natalia's dance partner. Cal is taller and leaner than Winston.

"I have to warn you, this is my first time line dancing, so I may not be very good."

"That's alright. I'll help you. Just follow my lead."

His left foot, across from my right, moves forward, causing me to step back. We alternate between right and left legs for four counts, then we take two steps back on each leg at a quicker pace for a four count, almost as if we are skipping. It takes me a few tries to feel comfortable with the steps, but I pick it up pretty quickly.

"Do you come here often?" I ask him.

"Every weekend," he replies with a smile.

"You must be a pro-dancer then."

"I'm not too bad," he says as he twirls me.

When the song ends, we thank each other for the dance. One of the line dances from our lesson earlier comes blasting through the speakers, and I line up next to Jocelyn and Paolo. I can see Gabi and Quin running toward the dance floor. They make their way through the crowd and line up next to us. We begin to move to the right, and then left, front, then back, ending with a few kicks before we change directions. I'm not surprised at how well Quin is dancing, but it is a bit of a shock to see him out on the dance floor. He must be trying to impress Gabi, who adds her own flavor to the line dance by rocking her hips with the steps.

When the song ends, a slow one begins to play. Gabi rushes off the dance floor toward the restroom. I look around, hoping someone will ask me to dance, but no one walks toward me. When I turn to walk off the dance floor, Quin is standing right in front of me. He smiles as he puts one hand on my waist. My right hand finds his left, and we begin to sway slowly to the music. "I didn't know you had a thing for older guys," he jokes, referring to the older gentleman whom I danced with earlier.

"It was just a dance," I say.

"So, who is this Jace guy?" he asks.

I was sitting next to Quin when Jace had called me at dinner. Quin must have seen the name on my caller ID. "He's the manager at the North Beach shelter," I reply.

"Why was he calling you on a Friday night?"

"Why does it matter to you?" I reply. He sounds jealous.

"Just curious."

I pause for a few moments before saying anything. "He called to let me know that I can transfer to the North Beach location next week."

"That's awesome! That's what you wanted, right?" Quin is smiling, but there is a hint of sadness in his tone.

"Yeah." I suddenly realize that if I move to my grandma's place, I won't be able to see him as often. It's probably a good thing, though, since he is dating Gabi now.

"I guess I'm just confused as to why he had to call you on a Friday night to tell you that." He seems to search my eyes for an answer, and I shrug my left shoulder. "Maybe he likes you?" he offers. I'm not sure what would give him the impression that Jace likes me. They have never met each other before, and I have never talked about Jace to Quin.

"Maybe he does," I respond matter-of-factly. "He sort of asked me out earlier today."

"Really?" Quin raises his eyebrows, then pauses before he adds, "You should go for it. It's been a while since you dated anyone."

His response stings a little. The fact that he is encouraging me to date someone else implies that he has no romantic interest in me. *Don't be silly*, I think to myself. *If he really wanted to date you, he would be dating* you, *not Gabi.*

"Maybe I will," I say as the song ends. I'm done playing the waiting game with Quin. We are probably better off as just friends anyway. But it's so hard to let go when you've liked someone for so long. I walk off the dance floor, brushing past Gabi on the way, heading toward the table we were at earlier. Natalia is sitting there with a few empty beer bottles. *How much are they drinking tonight?* I wonder.

"I got you a water," she says kindly, offering me the filled glass next to her.

"Thanks." I take a long sip.

As the night goes on, I dance a few times with Paolo and join in on the group line dances. When I'm not on the dance floor, I watch the advanced dancers. They make every move look so graceful and easy. Natalia looks like she is having the time of her life.

"This will be the last slow song of the evening, so ladies, grab a cowboy and get on out on the dance floor," the DJ eventually bellows over the speakers.

"Hey, Winston!" I shout. He is only a few feet away from me. "May I have the honor?" I ask, smiling.

"Yes, ma'am." He tips his hat. The strong smell of Scotch fills the air between us as he rambles on about how he misses living in Kentucky.

When the song ends, I head off the dance floor with Jocelyn and Paolo. "I have to get going, otherwise I'll never wake up for target practice tomorrow," Paolo says through a yawn.

"Yeah, me, too. It's getting pretty late," I say. Natalia, Gabi, and Quin walk over to us.

"I think I'm ready to head out, too," Gabi says. We all walk to the exit together, and then exchange hugs in the parking lot. The humidity has died down, and the air has cooled off a bit. "Abrielle, do you think you can drive Quin home since you live next door to him? Gabi asks.

"Sure," I reply, looking at him. He has his arm draped over Gabi's shoulder and is stumbling a bit, clearly intoxicated. As they kiss good night, I let the top roll down on my car.

Quin hops in the passenger seat, and I begin to drive home. I can see out of the corner of my eye that he has been staring at me for at least a solid minute.

"What?" I glance over at him.

"You looked really good out there on the floor tonight."

"Yeah, okay, drunken-stein," I say.

He laughs. "What do you think about Gabi?"

"She seems...nice. She's cute."

"Yeah, she is." He smiles into the distance.

I roll my eyes.

"Well, I'm glad you like her. Your opinion really matters to me."

The truth is, I don't know if I like her or not. "Want to drive to the shooting range together?" I ask, trying to change the subject.

"Mmmm, nah. I have an errand to run in the morning first."

"Yeah, if you're able to wake up before noon," I say. "You should drink some water before you go to bed."

"Okay, Mom."

I give him a look.

We pull up in front of my house. I push the button for the top on my car to roll up, and Quin quickly jumps out. I can't believe he doesn't even say good-bye, or thank you. The top meets the windshield, and I lock it closed. Just then my driver's door opens, and Quin bows, gesturing for me to get out the car.

"You are so wasted." I can't help but smile as I step out of the car.

"You're supposed to say thank you." A goofy grin stretches across his face.

I can smell the alcohol on his breath, and he's not even that close to me. "Thank you," I say.

"You're the best, Bri. Thanks for the ride home." He kisses my cheek and meanders off to his house.

I stand there on the sidewalk for a moment, confused, thinking about what just happened. I wipe away the moisture his lips left on my cheek. Why would he do that? Could he possibly be dating Gabi to make me jealous? *No, he's just drunk*, I answer myself, then start up my front steps.

My dad is lying on the couch. He must have fallen asleep while watching TV again. I turn the TV off, head up to my room, and set my alarm for 9 a.m.

Chapter 6

I'm about to head out the door the next morning when Ariana asks, "What are you up to today?"

"Target practice," I reply.

"I'm coming with you. Give me two minutes," she says, and runs off to grab her gun case.

"I thought you didn't like shooting guns," I remark as we drive to the range.

"Well, I'm not a huge fan, but I need to stay on top of my game."

"You're a second-degree black belt. I think you're on top of things," I say.

We pull up to the shooting range, grab our bags, and walk in. We sign in at the front desk and head to the lanes. Paolo and Quin are already here, and so is Gabi. *What is she doing here?* I think to myself. She'd said she was scared of guns. "Hi, Abrielle," Gabi says cheerfully.

"Hi, Gabi. This is my sister, Ariana," I say. Ariana holds out her hand, and Gabi shakes it politely.

"Do you work at the shelter, too?" Gabi asks.

"No, I'm going into my senior year of high school," Ariana replies.

"Oh, I thought you were the older one," Gabi says.

I try not to shake my head in annoyance. That comment makes me dislike her even more. I don't think my sister looks older than me at all.

We all line up in front of a target, except for Gabi. She drags a stool over and sits against the back wall behind Quin's lane. Paolo set up targets in the outline of a person, with red circles on the forehead and chest. I take my first shot, aiming for the chest. It hits the edge of the red circle. My second shot to the chest again hits the middle this time. Third shot to the head, right on the spot. It's been a while since I had come to target practice, but since I'm working security more often now, I'm determined to be accurate. I look around to see how everyone else is doing. Ariana has put one bullet through the target on the head, and the other two have come close. Quin's bullet holes were all to the chest area, with only one actually coming close to the target circle. Paolo had four bullet holes, all of which hit the chest target circle.

After a few minutes, Paolo waves to get everyone's attention, and we remove our protective ear wear. "Let's make a bet. We'll all start with fresh targets, and whoever can shoot the same spot in the center of the target wins. Best of five shots."

"Bring it on!" Ariana shouts.

"What's at stake?" asks Quin.

Paolo shrugs, then says, "Loser has to buy everyone lunch."

"Deal," I agree, intent to win.

We set our guns down while Paolo runs to change the targets. Quin shows Gabi how to stand when firing a gun, even though she isn't going to participate in the contest. It seems like an excuse for him to wrap his arms around her. "How long have they been dating?" Ariana whispers to me.

"About a month," I whisper back.

"I don't like her," Ariana responds.

"You've barely even talked to her," I say.

"I know, but there is just something about her I don't like."

"I'm not a huge fan, either, but she is a nice person as far as I know," I reply.

Paolo comes back to the lanes. "Who wants to go first?" he asks.

"I will." Ariana steps forward.

Her first shot hits the center circle. Her second shot misses the target, puncturing the paper a bit to the left. The guys smile at each other as if they knew she would mess up. She takes a deep breath. Her third, fourth, and fifth shot hit the same spot in the center circle. Four out of five. She turns around and smiles smugly. Gabi claps her hands. "Great job, Ariana!" she exclaims.

"Thanks," my sister replies as she steps back to watch the next person.

Quin steps up in the next lane. His first shot goes through the center target, but his second falls in the larger, outer circle, not even close to the first shot. "C'mon, babe, you can do it!" squeals Gabi. She is a bit obnoxious. Ariana looks at me and silently mocks Gabi. I stifle a laugh.

Quin's third shot hits the target again, but his fourth and fifth don't even come close. It's not like him to do this poorly in target practice.

"I'm glad I'm not your partner in the field," Paolo jokes as he punches Quin's arm.

"Funny," Quin mumbles as he walks over to Gabi.

"Better than I would have done," she offers, rubbing his arm in condolence.

"I'll go next," Paolo says as he walks into the next lane. His first shot hits the upper part of the center circle. He waits a few seconds before firing his second shot. It hits near the same spot. His third and fourth match up with the first shot, as well.

"No pressure!" I shout. He pulls the trigger, and his fifth shot misses the mark by two inches. "Not bad," I say as I walk past him to my lane. So far he has done the best as far as proximity goes.

As I hold my gun out, I think of all the reasons I want to hit the same spot five times in a row. First, to prove that I can protect those at the shelter. My first shot hits dead center in the middle circle. Second reason: to prove I can protect myself. My second shot hits the same mark. Third reason: to prove I can protect my family. My third and fourth shots hit the same mark. I take a deep breath. My last reason: because I have spent half my life dealing with cancer, because I'm a survivor, and because I can do anything I set my mind to do. The fifth shot hits the mark. I sigh in relief, and a smile spreads across my face.

"That's my sister, everyone!" Ariana shouts proudly.

"You should apply for the police academy," Paolo says. He's not the first person to suggest that. I've actually considered it, but I really like interacting with people in need. I'm minoring in criminal justice, though, just in case I change my mind.

"Good job," Quin says with a lack of enthusiasm, and Gabi nods in agreement.

"Well, I guess you can pick the place for lunch, since you're paying," Paolo says to Quin as he slaps him on the back.

"Good, then we can go to my favorite burger joint down the street."

"Don't worry. I think they have salads there, too," I say to Ariana as we head to the parking lot. She is a vegetarian. My phone starts to ring as we get in the car. It's Eva.

"Hello?" I answer.

"Hi, Abrielle. I was wondering if you could work security overnight. Cameron has a family emergency," Eva says. Cameron is one of the overnight security guards.

"Sure, I can do that. What time should I come in?"

"Midnight to six a.m. The other security guard will be okay from six to eight by himself."

"Who am I working with?"

"Holden. Thanks, I really appreciate it."

"No problem."

I have only seen Holden in passing toward the end of his shift. I have never really had a real conversation with him, and I've never worked with him before.

"You've been working a lot lately," Ariana says.

"Yeah, but I like being at the shelter. Plus I'm trying to save up a little bit," I say.

We walk into the burger joint. It smells like French fries and pickles. We place our orders and find a table in the back corner. "So, Gabi, have you lived in D.C. your whole life?" I ask in an effort to get to know her better, as Quin requested of me a few days ago.

"No, I grew up in Chicago. My family moved to D.C. a few years ago."

"I've always wanted to go to Chicago. What's it like?" I ask.

"There's no place like it in the world," Gabi replies with a sparkle in her eye. "The skyline is amazing, you can see it from miles away. There are tons of unique shops, many within walking distance of each other. The older buildings, with their grand architecture, tell a history of the city that is so magnificent, and despite the noise, it's always peaceful when you go for a walk along Lake Michigan."

I look at Ariana. "Maybe we can take a trip there over winter break this year."

"Oh, I would go during spring break," Gabi suggests. "Winters in Chicago can be very cold. You would enjoy it more in the spring."

"Maybe we can take a group trip," suggests Paolo.

"That would be fun!" replies Gabi. We both look at Quin. He shrugs.

"Sure," he replies and takes a bite of his burger. He has been pretty quiet all day. I wonder why he's acting so down. "Bri, your mom grew up in Chicago right?" he asks.

"Yeah she did. I wish we could have taken a trip there with her while she was alive." I look down at my phone and notice today's date. Suddenly, I realize that six years ago today, his mom walked out on him and his dad. He's had no contact with her since she left. He's only talked about it once, but every year on this day he seems to shut down. I've never really known how to console him. We both lost a parent, but my mom didn't *choose* to leave.

We finish our meals and move toward the door. "Well, I think I'm going to head to the pool the rest of the day. Does anyone else want to come?" Paolo asks.

Gabi looks at Quin and he shrugs. "Sure, we'll meet you there. I have to swing home and grab my bathing suit," she replies for both of them. The last thing I want to do is sit poolside and watch Quin and Gabi flirt all day.

"I think—" I start to say, but a yawn interrupts my reply. "I'm going to take a nap. I have to work an overnight shift later."

"Be careful," Quin says to me.

"I'll come to the pool!" Ariana cuts in. "I have my suit in my bag. You never know when you'll need it in the summertime!"

"Okay. You can ride with me if you want," Paolo offers.

I'm not really a fan of my sister hanging out with my friends, but it's not like she does it all the time. Ariana and Paolo hop in his car and take off. I turn to Quin and give him a hug. "See you later. Hang in there," I say, and he squeezes me harder. I can see Gabi over his shoulder open her mouth to say something, probably to ask why I made that comment, but I stare her down. She closes her mouth. She can talk to him about it later.

"'Bye, Gabi." I give her a quick hug, so that it doesn't seem awkward that I hugged Quin and not her, then head home.

Chapter 7

As I pull into the shelter parking lot, I survey the area. I have never been here this late at night before. I want to make sure no one is lurking in a corner. Maybe I'm just being paranoid, but I like to think I'm being cautious. I walk through the back door into darkness. There is one floodlight on in the cafeteria near the kitchen. The shelter looks eerie when it's dark and empty. The office door is propped open, and the light from the cafeteria shines onto the beige tiles in front of the doorway. As I approach, Holden appears. He is in his late twenties, with shoulder-length dark hair that is pulled back into a ponytail. "Hey, Abrielle," he says in a deep voice.

"Hi, Holden." I smile at him. He looks a little intimidating. He has a goatee, and he wears a security belt filled with gadgets around his waist. "This is my first overnight shift," I tell him.

"I know. Eva told me that you've been picking up shifts lately." He retrieves a belt from the desk next to him. "Put this on." Inside the pockets of the belt are a flashlight, a gun, a master key, and a walkie-talkie. Two security guards are staffed for every overnight shift. One usually makes rounds on the floor, while the other watches the security footage. "You can watch the cameras for the first few hours and I'll make the rounds," he says as I slip my ID lanyard around my neck. His tone isn't condescending like Silas's can be.

"I'm going to reset the building alarm now that you're inside," Holden says. "At night no one is allowed in or out of the building, not even to smoke. Don't open any exterior door, or the alarm will sound off and notify the police," he explains. "Making the rounds at night are similar to making rounds during the day. If you see anyone who looks suspicious inside or outside of the building, radio me and I'll provide backup," he says.

"Got it." I nod.

"Don't fall asleep," he adds with a wink, then leaves to start his rounds.

I sit down in the chair in front of all the security screens to watch over the building. This is going to be a long six hours. I stare at the screens. The security cameras are set to night vision, which creates a cool but somewhat creepy display. I can see Holden making his way down the hallway toward the sleeping quarters. It's really tempting to turn on my computer and respond to my e-mails. I feel like I can never keep up with them, especially since I get dozens per day from volunteer organizations that want to bring groups to serve at the shelter. It's hard to believe that Monday will be my last day here until my grandma recovers from treatment.

My thoughts take me back to my own cancer treatment. When I was first diagnosed, I thought that once treatment was over, I would feel okay and go right back to my regular activities. It took me eight months to regain my energy—and I had youth on my side. My grandma is pretty healthy, but I can't help but think it will take her even longer than that to regain her strength and energy after treatment. It saddens me to think about it, so I focus on the security screens instead.

After an hour, Holden makes his way back to the office. "It's your turn, newbie," he says as he sits down at my desk.

"So, you're the one who is always moving my stapler?" I joke.

"Yeah." He snickers as he picks it up and sets it down across the desk.

I walk out of the cafeteria into the hallway. The doorway to the upstairs offices is locked. There is no need to patrol that area. I continue walking to the front entrance and look out the glass double doors. When people are coming to provide different services, or to sign up for overnight stays, this is the door they come through. The sign-in desk is empty and the hallway is dark, but the exterior lights flood the lawn and sidewalk in front of the doors. I peer out the doors for a few moments, but I see nothing.

As I head toward the next hallway, I see movement out of the corner of my eye. A shadow moves across the lawn outside, too big to be an animal. I grab my walkie-talkie. "Holden," I speak into it. "Check the outdoor cameras. Do you see anything?"

"Hang on," he replies. I'm frozen in place as if whoever is outside will notice if I move. After what seems like forever, he replies, "I don't see anything."

"Okay. I just thought I saw someone." My senses are heightened.

"Probably a stray dog," he responds. I walk down the dimly lit hallway to the women's sleeping quarters and quietly open the door. Cots fill the entire room. Some women have blankets, and some don't. The shelter only provides cots for each person, not bedding.

Everyone appears to be sleeping, but I stand there a few moments to make sure. Then I head over to the men's dormitory farther down the hallway. I open the door and walk inside. There are not as many cots in here as the women's room tonight. There is a small light on near the bathroom. Lying in the stream of light is a guy in a T-shirt and boxers. I look away. The guy closest to me is wearing almost nothing, and suddenly I feel like I'm violating their privacy. There's no suspicious activity going on, so I leave and head back down toward the women's dormitory.

Suddenly bright lights start flashing along the ceiling in the hallway, and I realize it's the alarm system. There is no siren, just the bright lights to alert us. I panic and draw my gun, pushing myself back against the wall. I realize the alarm could have gone off simply because someone tried to exit the building. The rules are explained to the overnight guests each night, so they should understand that opening an outer door would cause the alarm to trigger. I'm not sure if I should secure one of the sleeping quarters or head back to the office. I grab my walkie-talkie. "Holden, what's going on?"

"I don't know. I'm locked in the bathroom!" He sounds angry. The public bathrooms near the office have several stalls, and they only lock from the outside, to ensure that no one locks themselves in.

Someone must have broken in, then, and if Holden is locked in, the intruder should be near the cafeteria. The worst part is, they can see me coming on the security camera if they are in the office. I decide to take my chances. Adrenaline rushes through my body, and I start sprinting back to the cafeteria, stopping before every corner to make sure no one is there. So far no one appears. I cautiously approach the cafeteria with my gun drawn. I can hear things being thrown around in the office. I take a step inside, and I'm immediately punched in the face near my left eye. The pain causes me to stumble backward, and whoever just hit me lunges for my gun with their right hand, but I'm too fast for them. I grab an arm of the intruder and hold the gun up in front of his chest.

"You win." He holds up his left hand in surrender. His voice is rough, and he smells like cigarettes.

I make the mistake of looking over his shoulder at his partner, who is running across the cafeteria toward the exit with something in his hand. His left hand swings up, knocking the gun out of my hand, and he kicks toward my shin, but I let go of his hand and jump back, missing the kick. He takes off running toward the exit. I pick up my gun and run over to the bathroom, unlocking the door to let Holden out. "They just ran out the exit," I say as I sprint to the doorway. I hear car tires squeal. When I get to the doorway, I can see they are at the edge of the parking lot. I shoot at the back tire, and they only continue a few feet before the tire goes flat. The two guys jump out of the car and take off running down the alley.

Holden runs up behind me. "Let them go. We have it all on camera," he says. "Did you see what they looked like?"

"No, he was wearing a face mask and a hat," I reply. My face is throbbing.

"You stay here and wait for the police. I'll go check the sleeping quarters to make sure everyone is okay. The police should be here soon, and they'll need to check the office for fingerprints, so don't touch anything."

"Okay." I stand in the doorway, thinking about what just happened. The cafeteria door had been busted open by the intruders, so there is no point in trying to close and lock it. Why would someone break into the shelter?

I stand in the doorway with my gun out until the police arrive. My mind is racing. Who were those people, and what were they looking for? To my knowledge this is the first time the shelter has ever been broken into. After a few minutes, the police finally pull up. A few of them walk around the exterior of the building to check the perimeter, and the rest come inside. Two of them head to the office to investigate, while two others approach me.

"I'm Officer Prost, and this is Officer McLelland," Prost says, gesturing to her partner. "Please have a seat," she offers, walking over to one of the tables. Her short red hair is pulled back into a stubby ponytail, and faint wrinkles stretch out from her eyes toward her hairline. Her bulletproof vest makes her look bulky. The officers sit across from me and pull out a pad of paper. "What's your name?" she asks.

"Abrielle Peregrine," I answer.

"You're Abrielle?" McLelland asks in surprise. He is a younger officer, with brown eyes and dimples. "I know Quin. I worked with him just last week," he adds.

I smile. Prost looks at McLelland sternly. I wonder how my name came up in conversation between the two officers.

"Can you describe the person who assaulted you?" Prost asks.

"I know he was a man, but he was completely covered. He was a little taller than me," I reply. A paramedic comes over and hands me an icepack for my face. "He reeked of cigarettes," I add.

"Who shot out the back tire of their car?" Prost asks.

"I did," I reply.

"Nice shot," McLelland says. "That car will help us track them down after we run the plates."

The officers ask me a few more questions, and then leave to question Holden.

Eva runs through the door toward me. "Abrielle, are you okay? I came as soon as the police department called me." She is wearing slippers, as if she'd run out of her house with the first pair of shoes she could find.

"Yeah, I'll be okay," I reply. "Why would someone break in? They were in the office looking for something."

"I'm not sure. We haven't had a break-in at all in the past year. We don't keep client records in the office. There's no money on the premises except for some petty cash. I can't figure out what they would take."

My head is throbbing, and I'm too tired to think.

"Why don't you go home and get some rest?" she offers. "I'll clean up here, and Silas will be in soon. Are you okay to drive?" she asks.

"Yeah, I can make it home," I reply. The eastern horizon is a lighter blue than the rest of the night sky; the sun is getting ready to pop out any minute. I hope that everyone is still sleeping when I get home. I don't want to talk to anyone.

Chapter 8

My eyes steadily open. Sunlight is trying to peek through my purple and gray curtains. I grab my phone to check the time. It's two in the afternoon. I slowly get out of bed and walk over to my mirror to check out my face. It's a little swollen where I got hit, and slightly bruised. I try to hide the bruise with some makeup. It doesn't completely mask what happened, but it'll have to do. I change my clothes and brush my teeth, then head downstairs.

When I walk into the kitchen, Ariana and Dad are sitting at the table playing cards. Someone has cleaned up this morning, because the counter isn't as cluttered as it normally is, and the tablecloth has been changed from one with pink and red flowers to an ivory-patterned one. Ariana's eyes grow wide when she sees me. "Who punched you in the face?" she asks in a cheeky tone.

Dad turns around in his chair. "What happened?" he asks, concerned.

"Two guys broke into the shelter early this morning while it was still dark out. They were rummaging through the office trying to find something. I'm pretty sure one of them saw me coming on the security cameras. I was making rounds, and when I turned the corner into the cafeteria, he was waiting for me."

"And then you let him know he messed with the wrong person, right?" asks Ariana.

"I tried, but he was stronger than me. He got away." I grab an icepack from the freezer and sit down with them at the table.

"You should have shot him as he was running away. There's no way you would have missed," she adds.

"He wasn't really a threat, and he didn't have a gun, otherwise I would have. I shot his car instead," I say with a grin.

"I can show you how to fight against someone who is stronger than you," she offers as she gets out of her chair to demonstrate.

"Maybe later."

"I'm glad you're okay," Dad says with concern. "When are you moving in with your grandmother?"

"I think I'm going to take some stuff over there today. That way I can go stay there, starting right after work tomorrow," I reply.

"I'm proud of you for giving up the rest of your summer to help her," he says. I shrug.

"It's not a big deal. I just want to be there for her."

"We'll come visit on the weekends," he offers.

I nod. I need to clear my head. "I think I'm going to take a walk," I say as I get up from the table. I grab some money and put on my sunglasses before heading out. The last thing I want is for people to stare at my bruise.

I begin heading down the street. The sunshine warms my skin as I walk. A few houses down, there are some little kids sitting on their front porch blowing bubbles. I smile as I remember what it was like to be that young and carefree, to not have any worries or stress. After three blocks of houses with the tiniest front yards, there is a strip mall. The sidewalk is crowded with people running Sunday errands. A group of teens sit outside a brightly painted table at the ice cream shop.

I walk past them, and the display in the window of the bookstore catches my eye. They have inspirational books set out. When I walk in, a little bell attached to the door makes a dinging sound. "Hello," the cashier says with a smile from behind the counter.

"Hi," I say as I walk over to the window display. The first book I see is a collection of encouraging quotes for cancer patients. I flip through it and read a few:

Don't waste your energy worrying. Use your energy to believe that you can win this battle.

Courage isn't having the strength to go on; it's going on when you don't have the strength.

Don't lose hope.

Focus on one day at a time, and make each day your best.

I decide to buy the book for my grandma. I take it over to the cashier to pay. He looks like he is still in high school. He is tall and lanky, with his blond hair gelled into a Mohawk. He looks at the book. "This has some really good quotes in it," he says.

"Have you read the whole thing?" I ask.

"Yep, I bought it for my aunt," he replies as he rings me up.

"Is she doing okay now?"

"We just found out she is in remission." He breaks into a huge smile.

"That's great news!" I respond, genuinely happy for his aunt.

"Thanks. I hope everything goes as well for whoever you are buying this book for," he says.

"Thank you. I hope so, too." I pay for the book and head back outside. It seems that everyone I meet knows someone who has dealt with cancer. It's way too common, and the fact that there still isn't a better way than chemo and radiation to stop it, frustrates me.

The scent of coffee and freshly baked cookies wafts down the sidewalk, and I walk toward my favorite coffee shop a few stores down. When I open the door, I see Quin standing in line. He looks so good in his police uniform. He looks over. "Hey, Bri," he says with a smile.

"Hi. Did you just get off work, or are you on your way in?" I ask.

"Just finished."

"Aren't you supposed to drink coffee *before* your shift?" I joke.

"I had a long day...and I heard you had a long night," he replies, bringing his hand up to gently touch the bruise on my face.

"Yeah, I did."

It's his turn to order. "I'll take a large iced coffee and whatever she wants," he says to the cashier as he steps aside so I can order. There's no point in refusing to let him pay; he'll just make a big scene about it. "A small coffee, and a blueberry muffin, please," I say to the cashier. "Thanks, Quin." We wait for the barista to hand us our drinks.

"What are you up to today?" he asks.

"I'm moving some things over to my grandma's house."

"I can help you. I don't really have anything going on."

"Okay, thanks."

"What time will you be ready to go?"

"Give me a few hours to pack."

"Alright, we can take my truck."

"Sounds good."

The barista hands us our drinks and my muffin. Quin holds the door open for me. "Do you want a ride home?" he asks. The summer air is hot and thick. I'm only a few blocks from my house, but I realize it might be difficult to eat a muffin and drink coffee while carrying the book I've just bought. I nod my head to Quin, and we walk toward his black pickup truck parked across the street.

*****

Almost two hours later, I have finally finished packing. I have two suitcases of clothes, a bag of toiletries, a container of shoes, and another bag with some music, books, and other miscellaneous items that I might want. I grab my favorite pillow and one of the suitcases and head downstairs. Quin is sitting on the couch with his feet up, talking to Ariana. When he sees me, he pretends to look at a watch on his wrist. "I thought you said you're free all day," I tease.

He grins, then gets up to get the rest of the stuff from my room. "Geez, do you want me to pack up your bed, too?" he shouts from upstairs.

"Can you? I know it will fit in the truck," I yell back.

Ariana jumps up from the couch to help, and we load everything into Quin's truck. "Mind if I come with?" she asks.

"Sure, why not?" I reply. We all climb into the truck and begin the drive to Grandma's house. "So, what did you hear about last night?" I ask Quin, curious to know if they've found the guys who broke into the shelter.

"Nothing about the break-in, but I did hear that the Pierce family is very wealthy, so maybe that has something to do with it." This is news to me. He looks over at me. "I'm glad you're okay," he says gently.

"If you find out who or why—" I start to say.

"I will let you know," Quin says, interrupting me and finishing my sentence. We sit quietly for a minute.

"I'm going to meet some of Gabi's extended family this week," Quin finally says, breaking the silence.

"Things are moving pretty fast then, huh?" Ariana says from the backseat.

"Yeah, I guess," Quin replies. "They live in Philadelphia. So we're driving up there Wednesday morning, and coming back Saturday."

"In time for the Natives game?" I say, more as a reminder than a question. He nods his head. "You forgot to order the tickets, didn't you?" I ask.

"I'll do that tonight," he replies with a grin. *I didn't know he was serious enough about Gabi to meet her extended family*, I think. "You must really like her," I say softly.

"I do," Quin replies sincerely.

I turn the radio on, and we listen to music for the rest of the ride.

Chapter 9

I open the front door to Grandma's house, and we all walk in with our hands full of my belongings. It sounds like someone is moving furniture upstairs. I shoot Ariana a puzzled look. "Grandma?" I shout.

"Just a minute," she yells back. We set my stuff down. The scent of fresh paint lingers in the air. The front curtains are open, and sunlight is streaming in onto the light hardwood floors. Her furniture is faded from the sun, and the same grade school pictures of Ariana and me hang on the living room wall. A piano is angled in the corner of the room, covered in a light blanket of dust.

Grandma walks down the stairs with Jace behind her. She is wearing a brightly colored sundress, and her long gray hair is braided to the side, hanging over her shoulder. "Hi, girls!" she exclaims before she reaches the bottom step. "And Quin! It's so good to see you!" she says with a smile.

"It's good to see you, too, Ms. Peregrine," Quin replies. We meet her at the steps for a hug. She seems winded. Jace is carrying a nightstand behind her. The sleeves of his T-shirt hug his biceps. I try not to stare. He sets the nightstand down. "Hey, Jace," I say with a smile.

"Hi, how are you, Abrielle?"

"I'm good. How are you?"

"Well, your grandmother sure is keeping me busy. Ariana?" he asks as he holds his hand out toward my sister.

"Yes." She smiles as she shakes his hand.

"Pleasure to meet you."

"So, you're *Jace*," Quin says. The way Quin says his name makes it sound like I talk about him all the time.

"So…you're Abrielle's boyfriend?" Jace asks, holding his hand out toward him with a friendly smile. Ariana snickers. They shake hands.

"No, definitely not," Quin replies, as he shakes his head. "We're just friends." *And that's clearly* all *he ever wants to be*, I think. I would rather have him in my life as just a friend, though, than not at all.

"Jace was just helping me turn the den into my new bedroom. I don't think I will be able to use the stairs much once I start chemo," Grandma says.

"Come see her new room," Jace says as he picks up the nightstand and walks down the hall with it. Her old den has been freshly painted a medium shade of blue that makes it look like a spa. The twin bed from the guestroom sits along one wall, and her long oak dresser takes up the other wall. "I wanted blue, because it's a calming color. Now I just need to go shopping to pick out a few decorative pictures for the walls. Maybe you can help me with that this week, Abrielle," she says.

"Yeah, I love to decorate," I say.

"Would you like to stay for dinner?" Grandma asks, looking around at all of us. "I won't take no for an answer," she adds.

"Sure, we would love to," Quin replies.

"I'll help you," I offer.

"Nonsense, I can do it. Go make some music for me on the piano while I cook." She gestures towards the living room.

"Okay. Just let me carry my things upstairs first," I say.

"I can help you," Jace says.

"Yeah, me, too," adds Quin, as if it's a competition to carry my belongings to my new room.

As the guys grab my stuff, Ariana whispers, "If you don't go for Jace, I will. He's insanely cute."

"Yeah, 'cause he would totally dismiss the fact that you're in high school," I whisper back. "I haven't even decided if I like him yet."

"You heard Quin in the car talking about Gabi. There's nothing in your future with him, so just go for Jace," she says. She's absolutely right. I just don't know if I want to date anyone right now.

We take my belongings upstairs to one of the three bedrooms. Luckily, the room I'm staying in is a neutral beige color, with hardwood floors. There is some contemporary artwork on the walls, and various shades of brown form circular patterns on the curtains. I helped Grandma decorate this room a few years ago. I'll unpack and rearrange the furniture tomorrow.

We head back downstairs, and I sit down at the piano and start playing. I haven't played since last summer, but my fingers remember what to do. I play a few songs from memory. When I stop, I hear clapping. Ariana, Quin, and Jace are all sitting on various couches, watching me. When I play, I get so caught up in the music that I forget about my surroundings. I get up and take a bow. "You're really good. Do you think you could teach me?" Jace asks as he looks into my eyes. "I've always wanted to learn how to play."

"Yeah, since we are practically neighbors now, I think we could arrange weekly lessons," I reply as I sit down next to him.

"Good. Mark your calendar, then, because I'm really serious about learning."

"Okay, I will," I respond, smiling. I didn't realize that Jace and I are still staring at each other until Quin coughs.

"So how long have you lived in the States?" he asks.

"A little over five years."

"What's it like in Great Britain?" Quin asks.

"Actually, we moved here from South Africa, which is where I grew up." I've always just assumed Jace's family was from England, too.

"South Africa? That's so cool!" Ariana exclaims.

"Well, I feel weird not helping with dinner. I'm going to see if your grandma needs anything," Quin says, and goes into the kitchen.

"Do you have a girlfriend?" Ariana suddenly blurts out, looking over at Jace.

He laughs at her bluntness. "No, I don't," he replies.

"What a coincidence. Abrielle is single, too!" she exclaims. I can feel my face turning red. Jace smiles at me.

Without knowing it, Quin saves me from the awkward moment when he yells, "Salads are ready!" from down the hall. Perfect timing. We all get up and walk into the kitchen. It smells like garlic bread and Italian herbs. Ingredients are scattered across the countertop.

As we all sit down at the kitchen table, Grandma says, "I'm making baked mostocolli. It should be ready soon." I love my grandma's cooking. She makes her own sauce with fresh herbs from her garden. I hope she can teach me how to cook while I live with her.

We pass the salad bowl around and begin eating. "Ariana, what have you been doing to stay busy this summer?" she asks.

"I'm teaching a Taekwondo class at the park district for kids, and hanging out with my friends," she replies as she stabs a cucumber with her fork.

"Oh, that sounds like fun. What age group do you teach?" she asks.

"Eight- to ten-year-olds." Ariana has always enjoyed martial arts more than me. She has been taking classes since she was ten. I was never that good at it.

"How long have you been teaching?" Jace asks her.

"This is my first summer at the park district. It's pretty cool," she replies.

"Maybe we can hire you for security at the shelter when you're done with high school," he adds.

"It would be cool to work there over the summer before college," she replies enthusiastically.

"Apparently, knowing how to fire a gun may be a skill you will need, too, so just master that and you will be good to go," Jace says.

"She's mastered that skill already," Quin says, through a mouthful of salad.

"I wouldn't say I've mastered it, but I'm pretty close," she says assuredly.

"Well, you Peregrine girls have a lot of hidden talents, don't you?" Jace asks.

"Yeah, we are pretty good at everything we do," Ariana replies jokingly. I smile.

"Your security guards need guns at the shelter? What could possibly happen that they would need a gun for?"

Grandma asks. I'm glad she hasn't noticed my bruise through the makeup.

"We had a break-in overnight during a security shift that I picked up, and it came in handy," I reply as I scoop up the last bite of my salad.

"Oh, are you okay?" she asks, her voice full of worry.

"In summary, one guy *tried* to beat me up, so I shot his car tire as they tried to escape," I reply. "By the way, Jace, did you find out why they broke in?"

"I know some paperwork is missing, but we have backup files on the computer. Thanks to your quick thinking, I don't think they found everything they were looking for. They saw you coming to the office on the security cameras, which probably scared them," he replies.

"Good," I respond.

"I'm going to find the guy who did that to you," he says, nodding toward my bruise. My face turns red. Quin looks over at Jace and rolls his eyes, but Jace doesn't notice.

The timer beeps on the oven, and Ariana gets up to take out the mostocolli and garlic bread. "Does anyone need a drink refill?" I ask as I get up to get more water.

Quin grabs his glass and rises from his chair. "I can get it, but thanks."

I turn the faucet on to refill my glass, and Quin stands next to me, shoulder to shoulder, as he waits to refill his own glass. I give him a look. "I'm pretty sure I'll find out who gave you that bruise before he does," he whispers as he leans in close. I don't reply. If he is serious about Gabi, then he needs to stop being so touchy-feely with me, because it's confusing to me and not fair to her.

After we sit back down at the table, Ariana walks around with the tray of garlic bread and gives us all a piece. Then she places the pan of mostocolli down in front of us.

"Jace, I heard you will start planning the charity ball soon. I can help you with phone calls to collect donations," Grandma offers. She looks like she is having a hard time catching her breath. I don't point it out, but I wonder if anyone else notices.

"That would be great," Jace replies as he scoops pasta onto his plate. "I'll get you a list of places to call."

"Mrs. P, is there anything I can do to help you during your treatment? Cooking, cleaning, anything?" Quin asks Grandma. She smiles at him.

"I can't think of anything at the moment, but I can imagine needing some help after a few treatments," she replies. "I'll have Abrielle let you know."

"Okay, well, I don't mind driving over here, if you need anything at all," he adds.

"Thank you Quin," Grandma says with a soft smile.

"I'm just two houses down, so feel free to call me, too," Jace adds. Quin gives him a look. I can tell he already doesn't like Jace.

After we finish dinner, I wrap up the small amount of leftover pasta. Jace and I clear off the table, and Ariana and Quin start to wash the dishes. "Grandma, I will come over after work on Monday. I'm only working a half day, and then I'll drive you to the hospital," I say.

"I'd like to drive for as long as I can," she replies. I know how she feels. There comes a point during chemotherapy when you no longer have the energy to do daily tasks, including drive a car. I was so weak at one point during my own treatment that even a gallon of milk was difficult to carry. I understand that Grandma wants to do what she can for as long as she can. "Okay," I respond.

"Thanks for dinner. See you tomorrow." I hug her good-bye.

Ariana leans over and whispers something to Jace, and he smiles and nods his head. Then she hugs Grandma good-bye, too. Quin and Jace thank her, we all say good-bye to Jace, then the three of us head home.

Chapter 10

As I finish getting dressed for my last day at the D.C. shelter, I can hear Dad getting ready for work. I woke up early so that I could see him before I leave. I gather my hair into a bun and walk downstairs into the kitchen. Dad is pouring coffee into a travel mug. "I'll take a cup please," I say as I open the refrigerator in search of something for breakfast.

"Good morning," he says. He looks energetic today. I don't like what I see in the fridge, so I take a banana from the counter and sit down at the kitchen table. Dad places a mug of coffee in front of me. "Thanks." I reach for the mug and take a sip.

"I was thinking I can come every other weekend to give you a break," he says.

"Okay, that sounds good."

"I wish your grandma would just move in with us during her treatment, but I already talked to her and she thinks she will be okay. She's so stubborn."

"Just like you," I say with a smile.

He lets out a sigh, then leans down and kisses my forehead. "'Bye."

"'Bye, Dad." I finish my coffee, then grab my bag, which contains a few things I forgot to pack. As I'm about to leave,

Ariana comes down the stairs, dressed in workout clothes. "Good morning," I say as she yawns.

"Morning," she replies as she sits down at the kitchen table.

"Hey, I was just curious—what did you whisper to Jace yesterday?" I didn't want to ask her in front of Quin, because I knew she wouldn't answer. A smile creeps across her face. "If I wanted you to hear, I would have said it out loud," she replies.

"C'mon, just tell me," I plead.

"I just told him that I hope you guys end up dating."

I let out a loud sigh. "You don't have to play matchmaker."

"He's cute, so why not give it a shot?" she asks.

"He's a few years older than me, and I don't think he would be interested in dating someone so much younger," I reply.

"He seemed into you. 'I want you to teach me piano so I have an excuse to sit close to you,'" she jokes in a deep voice.

I purse my lips. "I have to go."

"Have a fantastic day," she replies in a sarcastic tone.

I get into my car and roll the top down. It's still early enough in the day so that it's not too hot out. I'm driving right to Grandma's house after work, and I'm so glad I don't have to drive Ariana's car for the rest of the summer. I blast the radio the entire way to the shelter, and enjoy the warm air that swirls around me as I drive.

When I walk in, Sherina is sitting at the check-in desk. Her fingernails are painted to match her red V-neck shirt. "Surprise!" she says with a smile. I look around. Balloons hang from the ceiling, and a construction paper banner, clearly created by some of the kids, reads, "We will miss you, Miss P!" I can't help but smile. A few of the kids who are here regularly run over to me and give me a group hug.

"Hey, guys, I'm not leaving forever," I say to them.

"But we won't get to see you every day," Owen replies sadly.

"I know, but I will be here every Wednesday for meetings, so I will try to find you then and say hello each time, okay?"

"Okay!" they reply, grinning. I pull out an iPod charger from my back pocket and hand it to Owen before I head to the office. "Thanks, Miss P!" he exclaims and runs off.

I walk into the office to clock in. "You make it seem like I'm leaving the country," I say to Eva with a smile.

"I know you will only be gone a few months, but you will be missed, so all this is totally appropriate," she says with a huge smile.

"Well, thank you. It does make me feel appreciated." I put my ID lanyard on, then I work on my computer for a little while and make phone calls to confirm volunteers for the next few weeks.

I help the lunch volunteers set up their meal, and mingle with the guests who are waiting in the cafeteria. While it would be great to see them when I come back for charity ball planning meetings, I hope that things work out for them, and that they will no longer need the help of the shelter. I say my good-byes to the staff and everyone who is still in the cafeteria after the lunch crowd disperses. I will definitely miss being here with all the staff and regular guests whom I have become friends with.

I give Sherina a hug before I leave. "Stay in touch, and keep me updated about your grandma," she says.

"I will."

As I walk to my car, I notice someone smoking a cigarette along the side of the building. "Have a good day," I say as I squint in the bright sunlight.

"You, too. Good luck at the new location," the person replies. I can hardly see who it is, but the voice sounds familiar. I take a few steps toward him into the shade to see who I'm talking to. It's Vander. He is smoking a cigarette—and suddenly I realize that he was the one who broke into the shelter. I must look like a deer in the headlights, with my eyes growing wider by the second as I stare at him.

"Are you okay?" He throws his cigarette butt to the ground.

"It was you!" I yell loudly as I point at him. Why on earth would Vander break in to the shelter?

He takes off running toward an alley, and I chase after him. He's not too far ahead of me, but he keeps tipping over garbage cans, which slows me down a bit. As he runs into the second alley, I yell after him, "I just want to talk to you!" He continues to run. I grab my phone out of my back pocket and try to dial 911 as I chase him. The alley ends, and he turns left into a neighborhood. For a guy who smokes, he sure can run fast. I continue following him, hoping to catch up. I carefully dial the numbers as my phone shakes in my hand every time my foot hits the pavement.

Vander turns right, and the phone begins to ring. "Nine-one-one, what's your emergency?" an operator asks.

"I'm chasing one of the guys who broke in to the homeless shelter," I say. I look around for street signs to give her a location.

"Which direction are you heading?" she asks.

I was never good with directions. "I don't know. I just passed Grand and Mason Streets."

"Okay, just hold on. We'll locate you via GPS. Officers are on their way."

I keep the call connected, but I don't answer any more of her questions. I need to focus on Vander. The gap between us closes, and when I reach him, I push him as hard as I can. He stumbles and cries out in pain as his shoulder makes contact with the pavement. He rolls onto his back and grabs his left shoulder, wincing in pain. "Don't move," I say firmly.

Vander is breathing heavily. "Look, I didn't know you would be the one working the other night, and I wasn't trying to hurt you, Abrielle," he says.

"What were you looking for?" I demand.

"I wasn't looking for anything. Some guy hired me to come along with him. I thought it would be easy money. He said he was looking for cash, blank checks, and credit cards, and he hired me as a lookout. He knew I was familiar with the shelter."

I hear the sirens getting louder. "I'm sorry I pushed you down," I say. "I wouldn't have called the cops if you hadn't tried to run away."

Two squad cars pull up, and Quin and his partner rush out. Quin's partner begins to read Vander his rights as he handcuffs him. Vander's face contorts in pain with every movement he makes to stand up and walk to the car. "I think something is broken," he complains to the officer as he is pressed into the squad car.

"Are you okay?" Quin asks me.

"Yeah, it just happened so fast," I reply.

"Is this the guy who gave you the black eye?" he asks.

"Yeah, but I don't think he meant to," I say, knowing that Quin might try to take matters into his own hands with Vander.

"He hit you in the face, Bri. That doesn't just happen on accident," he says angrily.

"He is already hurt because I shoved him to the ground. Promise me you won't do anything more to him." Quin doesn't say anything, just looks at me. "Promise me," I beg.

"Fine," he huffs, and turns toward the driver's side of the squad car. "McLelland will take you back to the shelter in his car. Be careful," he says.

"No more overnight shifts?" I ask McLelland as I get into his car.

"Nope. Have you ever thought about becoming an officer? Shooting tires, self-defense, chasing down criminals, you would make a pretty good cop," he says.

"Maybe one day," I respond as I stare out the window. I can't stop thinking about what Vander said. I don't think the shelter has a lot of money in its bank account, so I'm not sure why someone would be looking for blank checks. Maybe he was looking for personal checks for the Pierces' account.

I wipe my forehead. I hadn't even realized I was sweating, because I was so focused on catching Vander. "So, how long have you and Quin been dating?" McLelland asks me.

I sigh. "We're just friends. He has a girlfriend named Gabi," I explain.

"Oh, he mentioned that, but he never said her name. He really seems to care about you, so I just figured it was you," he responds. We turn into the shelter parking lot and he stops the car. Why does everyone always think Quin and I are dating?

"I'm glad you're not dating him, because that means I can ask if you want to go to dinner with me tomorrow night," McLelland says. I wasn't expecting him to say that, and I'm flattered.

"I'm just starting to date someone, and I'm moving to North Beach, so now isn't the best time," I say. I feel bad because that is partially a lie. I'm really not dating anyone, but *maybe* I will date Jace someday.

"Well, if things don't work out with this other guy, here's my number," McLelland says as he hands me his business card. I smile at him to be polite. He's not a bad-looking guy, but I'm not interested in dating him.

"Thanks for the ride," I say as I open the door.

"Anytime."

Chapter 11

Grandma and I walk down the long, brightly lit hallway at the hospital to the oncology wing. The tile is mostly white, with an occasional gray one spaced here and there. Every few feet there is a scenic picture hung on the wall. They are spread throughout the hallway as if the hospital was trying to help you feel serene during your stay. Having experienced chemotherapy myself, I feel as if I am walking Grandma to death row. We turn the corner and walk up to the check-in desk. "Hello," the receptionist says with a warm smile. She is middle-aged and wearing gray scrubs.

"Hi, my name is Faustina Peregrine. I start chemo today," Grandma says.

"Okay, I just need your insurance card and a picture ID," the receptionist says politely.

Grandma reaches into her purse and pulls the items out quickly, as if she had them ready beforehand. She finishes checking in, and we find seats in the waiting room.

I look around. There is an elderly man in a wheelchair, wearing a baseball cap. Next to him is a younger woman with a cooler, probably filled with snacks and drinks for the long day at the hospital. Across the room sits a teenage girl and her mom. The girl's eyebrows are almost nonexistent, so I'm guessing she is the one battling cancer. One of the side effects of certain chemo drugs is losing your hair—all body hair. I would have never known she was wearing a wig if I hadn't noticed her lack of eyebrows. Seeing her causes memories of my past to flood my mind: sitting in the waiting room, impatiently waiting for a nurse to call my name. The oncology wing was the one place where I wasn't self-conscious about my appearance, because I knew that everyone else there was going through the same thing.

"Ms. Peregrine," a nurse calls from across the room. That was quick. We get up and walk across the room. The nurse leads us to a small room with a curtain instead of a door. "We will be drawing blood before every chemo treatment to check your counts," the nurse states. "You will always come back here first, then wait about twenty minutes for us to review the results before starting treatment," she adds.

"Okay." Grandma . I take her purse as she sits down. "It's still a little swollen around your port site," the nurse says as she gently feels the port on Grandma's left side. I hated having a port. It is a little device about the size of a half dollar that connects to a vein in your upper chest. It is used to draw blood, and for chemo infusions.

"When did you get that?" I ask her.

"Your dad took me the other morning," she replies.

The nurse draws her blood, takes her weight and blood pressure, and goes over a list of questions with her. Then we are directed to a different waiting room, closer to the infusion rooms. This waiting room is smaller, with a TV mounted on the wall. It's not as crowded here, but there are the same green-colored chairs and stacks of various magazines on a table in the corner. A poster on the wall catches my attention. It's about a program for survivors to mentor cancer patients. I stare at the poster, intrigued. I wish they'd had a program like that when I was going through treatment.

"You should sign up for that," Grandma says, interrupting my thoughts. "You have a lot of experience to share with other people."

"I don't know. Maybe." Right now I want to focus on helping my grandma, but I do like the idea of being able to help others during their treatments, too.

After a little while, another nurse calls us into the infusion room. In the center of the room is the nurses' station. A male and a female nurse sit at the desk answering phones and responding to beeping machines. There is a large open space where people sit on recliners, hooked up to machines, and along the right side of the room are four private rooms. "We will put you in a private room today, since infusion will take four to five hours," the nurse says as she leads us to the first room.

She pulls back the curtain. There is a small TV on one wall next to a small storage cabinet. A recliner sits along one wall, with a small chair on the third wall and a swivel stool for the doctor. Grandma sits in the recliner, and the nurse hooks a bag of liquid to an IV stand next to the chair. "When the bag gets low, the machine will beep to alert a nurse, and we will come change it. Today's infusion will take longer so that we can make sure you don't have an allergic reaction to any of the medicines," the nurse explains.

"Okay," Grandma says. She looks positive. I was so scared for my first treatment.

I remember falling asleep every time I received chemo. It made the time go by faster to just sleep through it. I'd brought a book to read in case Grandma falls asleep today, and I was right—after twenty-five minutes, she is out. After a few hours of reading, I go to the pharmacy to pick up her anti-nausea medicine. Memories of throwing up on the car ride to the hospital play back in my mind like a terrible movie. When I first started treatment, I didn't take the anti-nausea medicine until I actually felt nauseous, but by that time it was too late. I will make sure Grandma takes it right away for the first few days regardless of how she feels.

As I'm walking back after a trip to the restroom, I pass by a few patients receiving treatment. An African American women is reclined in her chair, sleeping. A middle-aged man next to her is reading a newspaper, while a younger guy in his twenties plays on his phone next to him. The teenage girl from the waiting room is the last person before my grandma's room. I try not to stare, as I remember during treatment I hated when people stared at me. I always wondered what they were thinking. Sometimes I felt like they were judging me; other times I felt like they thought I looked weird without hair. As I am about to turn away, the girl's eyes catch mine, and I smile sympathetically.

"I like your shoes," she says.

"Thanks," I say. There's nothing really special about my shoes. I'm just wearing my pink and black sneakers. For some reason I feel compelled to talk to her. "What are you battling?"

"Lymphoma."

I walk over to her and sit in the empty chair next to the woman I'm assuming is her mom. "I kicked lymphoma's butt..." I do the math in my head. "It will be three years ago this week! And I can tell by the look in your eyes that you're going to kick its butt, too."

She smiles and nods. "I'm Felicity, and this is my mom, Vivian." Vivian's brown hair is streaked with blond highlights, and glittery designer earrings dangle from her ears. I hold out my hand to shake each of theirs.

"I'm Abrielle. I'm here with my grandma, who is battling lung cancer."

"Abrielle," the nurse interrupts us. "Your grandma is ready to go home now." I nod my head at the nurse and stand up.

"Well, I'm here at this time every week, so feel free to come visit me if you're here," Felicity says.

"Okay, I will," I say kindly. I don't know her at all, but somehow I feel connected to her. I feel like all cancer patients share a bond that no one else will ever understand. As soon as we are diagnosed, we become part of an unspoken family of fighters, united in hope and strength.

I walk toward my grandma's room as the nurse brings us a wheelchair, insisting we need to use it in case she gets dizzy on the way to the car. Grandma reluctantly gets into the chair, and I push her out to the parking garage. "How do you feel?" I ask, recalling it takes a couple of hours for the drugs to penetrate your system.

"I feel normal, just a little tired," Grandma replies. *Enjoy the feeling of normal while it lasts*, I think, knowing all too well that after a few weeks, the side effects will be in full swing. It's dark outside when I pull out onto the street.

Grandma falls asleep on the drive home, and I feel bad waking her up to go inside the house. She looks strong, but I know the chemo pumping through her veins will physically weaken her body over the next few days. I get her situated in her room, with a garbage bag in case she gets nauseous, and place a glass of water on her nightstand.

"Good night, Grandma," I say, but she has already fallen asleep. I didn't do much today physically, but I am emotionally exhausted. As I head upstairs to my room, my phone rings. "Hi, Dad," I say.

"Hey, how did everything go today?" he asks.

"We didn't spend much time in the waiting room."

"That's always a nice surprise," Dad replies.

"She just went to bed."

"Take good care of her."

"I will."

"Call me tomorrow night."

"Okay, good night."

"'Night."

I get ready for bed and turn out the light. The moonlight streams through the window. I stare at the ceiling for a while before falling asleep. This is the second time I have had to watch someone I love battle cancer. But this time I'm old enough to help—and to understand what's going on. Grandma's positive attitude gives me hope that she really can win this battle, but I know too well that it is a very difficult journey. Mom had a positive attitude, too, but she didn't make it. Tears roll down my cheeks as I think of my mother. Lost in memories of her, I drift off to sleep.

Chapter 12

I decide to go for a run after dinner. I scribble a note in case Grandma wakes up from her nap, and I place the phone, along with her meds and a glass of water, on her nightstand, then tiptoe out of her bedroom. I slip my phone into my pocket, put on my sneakers, and head out the door. I stretch a little bit on Grandma's front lawn as I take in my surroundings. Not many cars are parked on the street, as most houses here have driveways. There is a purple Challenger in front of Jace's house, and a red minivan down the street. The thing I love about Grandma's neighborhood is that no two houses look alike; they all vary in color and design. The houses were built in the early 1900s, so they have a lot of character. Some are brick ranches, while others are two-story homes. Each house has a different color of brick or siding from the next one. Some have arched doorways, while others have decks off the front doors.

I run for about twenty minutes, then I turn around and run back. I don't want to wander too far away from the streets I am familiar with. When I get back, Grandma is still sleeping, so I decide to water the flowers before I shower. I walk down the porch steps to the hose and fill up her green watering can.

As I walk around the front of the house, the sun begins to set. I never realized how many flowers and plants decorate

Grandma's yard until now. Gorgeous red, white, and pink flowers grouped together in ceramic pots are scattered around the porch, while bushes and flowering plants wrap around the house from front to back. I finish watering them, then go inside.

Grandma is sitting in the kitchen, eating the chicken and salad I'd set aside for her. "How was your nap?" I ask her.

"I feel better now," she replies.

"Don't forget I have a meeting tomorrow in D.C."

"I remember. I'll be okay." I pour myself a glass of water, while Grandma goes on. "I was thinking that while you are here, we could clean out my house, reorganize, and de-clutter. It would give us something to do, and I've been meaning to do it for a while," she says.

"Okay, just let me know which room you want to tackle and when," I say. I doubt she is going to have the energy to actually go through her entire house and reorganize things, but if she wants to try, I will help.

"Do you want to watch a movie?" I ask.

"Sure," she replies. We go into the living room, and I pick out an old black-and-white movie. I'm not a huge fan of older movies, but there are a few good ones, and Grandma really likes them. I make some popcorn, turn the overhead light off, then sit down on the couch next to Grandma. We watch the movie until we can no longer keep our eyes open.

*****

I walk into one of the meeting rooms at the D.C. shelter for the charity ball planning meeting. The room is set up with tables and chairs arranged in the shape of a rectangle, like a large conference room. A dry-erase board hangs on one of the light beige walls, and a few inspirational quotes decorate the room. I am ten minutes early, but Jocelyn and Jace are already there. I convinced Jocelyn to help out this year. "Hey!" I say as I walk farther into the room.

"Hello, love," Jocelyn replies. I smile at her. I never went to planning meetings last year, but I think they will be more fun with a friend.

"Hi, Abrielle. I'm glad you were able to make it," Jace says. "I will be right back. I'm going to go grab some beverages for the meeting."

"Do you need any help?" I ask.

"I think I can handle it, but thank you for offering" he responds.

As soon as he walks out, Jocelyn turns to me and says, "Oh my gosh, he is so cute!"

I smile. "I know!"

"Well, I heard about the plane ride you are going to take in a few days, so I hope you will just go for it with him," Jocelyn says.

I fidget before responding. "I'm thinking about it," I say. Jocelyn can sense my hesitation.

"Abrielle, don't pass up on dating him because you are waiting for Quin. Quin hasn't taken any action in telling you how he feels. You shouldn't need to convince a guy that you're worth dating. Instead you should date a guy who is already convinced you *are* worth dating, and Jace seems convinced. His eyes lit up when you walked into the room," she says.

I sit up straighter in my chair. She's right. I do want to date Jace, but a small part of me has been still hanging on to the idea of going out with Quin.

A group of people walk into the room, ending our conversation. Eva, Dalilah, two men, and a young woman whom

I have never met before begin to assemble around the table. "Hi, I'm Luke. I'm a board member," says a shorter man with glasses.

"I'm Abrielle, and this is Jocelyn," I reply as we shake hands.

"Isaac," a younger guy with shaggy brown hair introduces himself.

"I'm Reagan," says a girl who looks to be my age, with black and purple hair. Her hair is longer on one side than the other, framing her face. "I like your bracelet," she says to Jocelyn, who is wearing a black and brown leather braided bracelet.

"Abrielle!" Dalilah exclaims as she throws her arms open for a hug. Dalilah became pretty good friends with my mother before she passed away. We used to volunteer here regularly when Dalilah first opened this location, so she got to know my family pretty well. "I can't wait to have you start at the North Beach location tomorrow night," she adds.

"I'm looking forward to it!" I have never been at the North Beach location before. I imagine it's a pretty similar setup.

We all find seats around the table. I sit next to Jocelyn, and Dalilah sits at the head of the table. She takes out a few papers from her portfolio and hands them to her right to be passed around. Jace comes back with the beverages and hands them out before sitting down across from me, next to Reagan.

"Thank you all for coming today," Dalilah begins. "This will be our fifth annual charity ball. The two biggest tasks for this event are soliciting items for the silent auction and selling tickets for the event. We will need to recruit a few more people for the committee, so if you know of anyone who might be interested, please invite them to next week's meeting."

"Maybe you should invite Gabi. Didn't she say she wanted to help out here?" Jocelyn whispers jokingly to me. I shake my head and try not to smile.

Dalilah continues, "Let's figure out which subcommittee we each want to be a part of first. Reagan, you did a great job designing the posters last year. Would you be able to do that again?"

"Sure," she replies.

"Good, so you will be a part of marketing. Does anyone else want to be a part of the marketing team? This involves contacting radio stations, hanging up flyers within the community, and contacting groups to invite them, among other things."

"I can help with that," Jocelyn responds. She is really outgoing, so she is a good fit for those kinds of tasks.

"Good. You and Reagan can meet later, and divide up the work. Abrielle, last year you helped collect donations. Would you be on the silent auction committee?"

"Yes," I reply. I'm sure being on the committee entails more than simply picking up the donations from donors like I did last year.

"Great. You and Jace will be working together then. You may need to recruit a few other people to help you." I look at Jace across the table, and he smiles at me. I'm glad we will be working together more. This will give me a chance to get to know him better.

"I'd like to be a part of the silent auction committee, too," Isaac volunteers.

"Okay," Dalilah replies as she adds that to her notes. "So, Eva and Luke, that leaves you with what I like to call the operations committee, is that okay?" They both nod.

"What is that committee in charge of?" Jocelyn asks. It sounds important.

"Finding a band, recruiting volunteers to work the ticket table, picking the menu, and other miscellaneous things that will make the event run smoothly," she replies.

Jocelyn nods her head.

"You will notice at the top of your agenda I've listed the event location, time, date, and ticket price. We can seat up to three hundred people in the ballroom, so I would like to fill all the seats this year. Last year we only sold two hundred and fifty tickets." Dalilah doesn't waste any time in going over the details and finding people to complete the tasks. After a few minutes we break up into subcommittees, spreading out throughout the room.

Jace, Isaac, and I sit at one corner of the table. "So, I heard you're a hero around here," Isaac says to me. Jace smiles and flips to a clean page in his notebook.

"What are you talking about?" I ask with a perplexed look.

"You know, chasing down some guys who broke in to the shelter, shooting out their back tire, then breaking one of the thieves' collarbones a few days later."

"Vander broke his collarbone?"

"No, *you* did that, when you pushed him down after chasing him," Isaac says with a grin. "I'm pretty confident in a fight because of my size, but I think I'm going to try to stay on your good side," he says playfully.

"Yeah, well, it's probably in your best interest not to make me mad," I reply jokingly.

"He's going to have a lot of opportunities to get on your good side, since you will be working security together," Jace chimes in.

"Well, out of all the security guards I have worked with, I think you're my favorite so far, and I have only known you for, like, forty minutes," I say.

Isaac elbows Jace. "Did you hear that? I'm her favorite?"

"Yeah, well, let's see if she is still saying that after a few days of working with you." Jace grins. "Anyways, we have a lot to figure out today, so let's focus." His demeanor has shifted into a leadership role. I've never sees this side of him before. I like it.

Jace pulls out a list of places that have donated in the past, and gives us each a copy. "We will need to call these places and see if they can donate again," Jace says. We brainstorm for a few minutes about different businesses and organizations that we can solicit help from that aren't on the list, then divide them up among the three of us to call. I leave the meeting with a great amount of phone calls to make.

Jocelyn and I walk to our cars together.

"How's Reagan? She seems pretty cool," I ask.

"She definitely knows what she is doing. She's a little opinionated, but she seems like she would be fun to hang out with."

"Maybe we should invite her out sometime."

Jocelyn nods her head. "I'll see ya later."

"'Bye."

When I get to my car, I check my cell phone. I have text messages from both Quin and Dad. The one from Dad reads, "Stop over at the house after your meeting. There's a package on the kitchen table for you." *I didn't order anything online, so what the heck is in the package?* I wonder. The text from Quin reads, "Hey, can we meet up when you get off work?" I wonder what he wants. I hit Reply: "I am heading to my dad's now. Just got out of a meeting."

Quin is waiting for me on the front steps when I pull up. I get out of my car and walk toward the front door. "Congratulations," he says with a big smile. I stop for a moment and think. Then my eyes grow wide and I exclaim, "It's been exactly three years!"

"Yep, and we're going out to celebrate!" he says. Three years ago today, I got a phone call from the oncologist saying I was in remission. I usually celebrate every year with my family and Quin, but I have been so busy with my grandma this time around that it has totally slipped my mind. It feels so good to think that I have been cancer-free for three whole years!

"Let me just get a few things from inside, and then we can go," I say. I open the front door, run up to my room to grab a few scarves for my grandma that I'd forgotten to pack, and grab the package from the table.

"What's that?" Quin asks.

"I'm not sure. It's from my dad," I reply. It's a small box, wrapped in shiny silver paper with a lime green bow.

"Open it," Quin insists. I set the scarves and my keys on the coffee table, then slide the bow off. I rip through the wrapping paper and open the box. It's a necklace in the shape of an awareness ribbon, with lime green crystals. There's a note that says, "A hero is an ordinary individual who finds the strength to persevere and endure in spite of overwhelming obstacles. —*Christopher Reeve*. You're my hero. Congrats on three years cancer-free and going strong. Love, Dad."

Tears well up in my eyes as I smile at the necklace. It's perfect. Quin comes up behind me and fastens it around my neck. "Thanks," I say as I turn around to hug him. I am overwhelmed with different emotions. I feel lucky to be alive. I feel strong for surviving. I feel hope for my future. I feel worry for my grandma—and sorrow that my mom and countless others didn't survive.

"Okay, c'mon, I don't want to be late for the appointment," Quin says lightly as he brushes away a tear from my cheek.

"What appointment?" I ask.

"You'll see," he says, leading the way to his truck. Quin has never been comfortable when people get emotional.

I call Dad once we get in the truck to thank him. I look out the window as we talk. I recognize the streets we drive down, but I have no idea where he is taking me. Finally we pull up in front of an ice cream shop. We hop out of the truck. "Ice cream?" I ask.

"Nope. This way." We walk down the street a short ways, and he pulls open the door of a tattoo parlor.

"Ummm, I'm don't think I want a tattoo," I say.

"You don't have to get one, but I'm going to."

I'm confused. Why would he bring me to a tattoo parlor to celebrate my cancer remission? "Hey, Quin," the guy at the front counter says.

"Hey, Landon," Quin says. Colorful tattoos spread from the guy's neck down to his arms, and his lip is pierced. He reaches into a file folder, pulls out a sketch, lays it on the counter, and then walks away.

"This is what I'm getting finished on my right arm today." Quin points to the sketch. I look down, stunned. It's a picture of two boxing gloves hanging on a brick wall. One glove is outlined in lime green, with the lime green lymphoma awareness ribbon across it, and the other glove is outlined in yellow with a yellow lung cancer awareness ribbon curling around. In the top corner of the brick wall, written in white across the bricks, is the word Hope in graffiti lettering. In the opposite bottom corner is the word Strength.

"Wait, what do you mean, you're getting this *finished*?" I'm confused.

Quin pulls his three-quarter-sleeved shirt off to reveal what the tattoo artist has accomplished in the first session. It starts just under his shoulder and comes down mid-bicep, then wraps around his arm. "I've always wanted a tattoo. And you have been through so much, but handled everything so well, that it inspired me to sketch this. The gloves symbolize your fight with cancer. Obviously the ribbons represent you, your mom, and your grandma's battle. I just liked the addition of the words on the wall, because witnessing what you all went through gives me strength in difficult situations."

I am in shock. I never could have imagined in a million years that anyone would want to get a tattoo that has anything to do with me. "This is a pretty big tattoo," is all I can think of to say.

"I wanted to put it somewhere that I can see it every day as a reminder that I can overcome any difficulties, just like you."

I run my hand over it.

"I can't think of a better image to put on my body," he adds as he stares deeply into my eyes. I want to forget everything that Jocelyn said earlier about moving on, and kiss him right now, but I fight the urge.

"Everything is set up," Landon says as he pokes his head out from behind a curtain, interrupting my thoughts.

"Do you want to watch?" Quin asks. I hate the sight of needles, but I have never seen anyone get a tattoo before.

"Okay," I reply hesitantly, and we walk to the back room.

There are three chairs set up for customers, each divided by a black curtain that can be pulled shut for privacy. A large mirror hangs on one wall, and pictures of tattoos cover the walls. Quin sits down and rests his right hand on the padded arm of his chair. I sit down next to him. Landon slides over on a roller chair and swipes the tattoo site with an alcohol wipe. He looks at my necklace and says, "So you're the girl." I can't help but smile. "How long have you been together?" he asks as he picks up the tattoo gun.

"We're not," Quin replies. I can feel my cheeks growing warm.

"Had me fooled. Dude, I can try to turn this into something else," he says to Quin jokingly. If one more person says something about us being together, I might lose it.

"Does Gabi know you're getting this?" I ask Quin.

"No," he replies nonchalantly.

"Is Gabi your girlfriend?" Landon asks.

"Yeah," Quin replies casually.

"My guess is she won't be for long when she finds out you're getting a tattoo that has to do with another girl," he says. I wonder how Gabi will respond, and why Quin hasn't told her yet. If I were dating a guy who got a tattoo like this about another girl, I would question his feelings toward her. Suddenly, anger creeps over me and I stand up. "I'll be right back," I say hastily as I storm out of the room.

Quin looks concerned. "Are you okay?" he calls after me, but I ignore him.

I step outside into the sunlight and want to scream, but there are people walking by. What is the point of this tattoo? Quin said it was to help him in difficult times, but how can he look at it and not think of me every time? Why would he want a constant reminder of me on his arm, when we aren't even dating? I must look like a lunatic pacing back and forth in front of the tattoo parlor, fuming. Maybe Quin wants to break up with Gabi and he's hoping that when she sees this tattoo that will be the end of it. I take a deep breath. When I think about it, I'm actually flattered that he is getting this done, but I can't help but wonder if he's trying to play some mind game with me. I can't keep entertaining the idea that I will one day be with him. It's driving me crazy.

I take another deep breath. Maybe I am just over thinking things. He's already explained why he is doing this. I don't know if there are deeper motives behind it, but I feel like I have a really good chance with Jace, so I'm not going to consider a relationship with Quin anymore. Resolved, I take a deep breath and walk back into the tattoo parlor.

"Are you okay?" Quin asks again when I enter the room, staring at me with a concerned look on his face.

"Yeah, I just...got nervous about the needle. You would think after everything I've been through I would be used to needles by now," I lie. I can't tell him why I really stormed out. It would be awkward. Landon is concentrating on the tattoo, and the gun hums in his hand.

I sit back down. "Does it hurt?" I ask him.

"Not really," he replies. Part of me wishes it *would* hurt, after all the confusion he has put me through. A movie is playing on the TV that is mounted to the wall in front of us. We sit in silence and watch the screen as the artist continues to work.

An hour later, the tattoo is finally finished. "Alright, man, you know the rules," Landon says, handing Quin a few packets of ointment.

"Thanks." Quin shakes Landon's hand.

"It was nice to meet you," Landon says to me.

"You, too," I say with a polite smile.

"And now, if you want ice cream, we can go," Quin says.

"Nah, but thanks. It's been a long day, so I think I'm going to head home."

"Okay," he replies as we get into his truck. "You think you would ever get a tattoo?" he asks me as we begin the drive back to the house.

"I'm not sure...but I don't think so. I like them on other people, but I don't think I could decide what to get or where." I stare at Quin's right arm. His shirtsleeve is still rolled up, exposing his bicep. "It turned out really nice," I add.

"Yeah, I think so, too," he says with a smile. "Before I forget, this is for you." He reaches into his backseat to grab something. He hands me a picture frame with a sketch of the tattoo in it. "To the strongest person I know."

"Thank you," I say with a fake smile. I don't feel strong right now. I just feel confused. I try to bury all my questions about the real motives behind his tattoo. It's a waste of my time to think about them.

Chapter 13

"Welcome to the North Beach Shelter," Jace says to me as he holds the front door.

"Thanks," I say, smiling back at him. This location already seems much different. It is a little bigger, and it has a large parking lot in the front of the building, unlike the D.C. location. I walk in and a receptionist greets me.

"Hello, welcome to the shelter. I'm Karyn," she says with a warm smile. A black headband pulls her short gray hair back from her face.

"Hi, I'm Abrielle, the transfer," I say. I hope I can remember everyone's name.

"Nice to meet you. The front office is right here," she says as she opens a door behind her. There is a large two-way window on the wall behind her desk.

"Thanks."

The office is much larger than the one in D.C. There are desks divided by a short partition right when you walk in for clients to talk to staff about aid. Behind those desks are three more desks. A middle-aged woman sits at one of them, tapping away on her computer keyboard. Dalilah walks out from a private office in the back of the room. "Hello, Abrielle," she says excitedly.

Isaac pops his head out from behind a wall that extends to the middle of the room. "Hey there," he says to me, then disappears again. I wonder what's behind the partition.

"Hi, Dalilah," I say as I walk toward her.

"Here is your ID." She hands a lanyard over to me.

"And here is your gun and holster in case you need to save the day again," Isaac says as he steps out from behind the partition and hands them to me. He goes back over to a small safe and closes it. I'm guessing the guns are kept in there. Behind the partition are two computer stations, a phone, and a slew of TVs displaying security footage. "Welcome to your new workstation." Isaac swivels an empty chair.

"Security procedures are pretty similar at both locations," Dalilah says to me.

"Isaac, can you give her a tour? I have some things to take care of."

"Sure thing," he replies.

As we walk past the desks, the middle-aged woman is on the phone. "This is Tia," Isaac says. She smiles and waves. When we get to the front reception area, you can only go right, through a set of glass double doors, down a hallway. The hallways here are painted with murals of people laughing, playing instruments, and helping each other. "The doors we just passed through stay locked at night. This door to the right is the women's room, and up ahead is the men's room. To the left are the showers and restrooms," Isaac says as we continue down the hallway. At the end of the hallway is a door that sunshine pours through.

"Is that an entrance?" I ask as I point down the hallway.

"No, but there is a small grassy area out there where kids can play, as well as a section for smokers. It's a fenced-in area that you can only enter from the inside of the building," Isaac replies. *Just like the D.C. location*, I think.

We approach a door on the right, after the bathrooms, and walk through. "This is the cafeteria and the kitchen." The room has windows along one side near the ceiling, where more light streams through. A check-in desk is stationed in the far corner near an entrance, just like at the D.C. location. Everyone who comes for a meal or to spend the night must sign in at that desk. The air-conditioning chills my body. It seems to be colder in this room than in the rest of the building, and it doesn't smell like a gym locker. A few people are sitting around playing cards or watching TV.

"C'mon," Isaac says as he walks toward the check-in desk. I follow him. "Abrielle, this is Giselle," he says, introducing me to the girl working at the desk. She has wavy blond hair and wears purple-framed glasses.

"Hello," she says as she holds out her hand for me to shake. "We don't have as much suspicious activity here as you do at the D.C. location, but I feel safer knowing you're working here," she says. *Has everyone heard about what happened?* I wonder.

"What I did wasn't a big deal. I was just doing my job," I say.

"Well, from what I heard, you did it pretty well," she comments.

"Thanks."

"Alright, let's finish the tour, Little Miss Celebrity," Isaac says as he heads toward a door that leads to the kitchen.

"Abrielle! Welcome to North Beach!" Reagan exclaims. "I was just finishing up inventory before I head home," she adds with a clipboard in her hand. She is wearing black skinny jeans with a form-fitting purple top. I never liked doing inventory at the D.C. location.

"Do you need any help?" Isaac offers.

"No, I'm almost finished," she says.

Good, I think. I didn't want to help with inventory anyway. But Isaac looks a little disappointed that she's said no.

"Alright, then. See ya later," Isaac says.

The kitchen is set up the same way the D.C. location is. There is a huge walk-in freezer in one corner, two stoves, and a double-stacked oven, all in a row down the wall, next to the freezer. Then there's a huge cupboard for pots, pans, utensils, and storage. The next wall is lined with two industrial fridges and a door, which Isaac points to.

"This door leads back to the offices," he says. "Straight ahead is a small conference room where we have our staff meetings, and this is Reagan's desk." Stacks of paper are strewn all over the surface. Reagan seems a bit disorganized. All of her office supplies are purple. That must be her favorite color.

"And this is Jace's desk," Isaac says as we walk past it back to the security area. His desk is kept very neat. There is a picture of him next to his computer with his parents standing in front of a plane. He must have just left for the day.

"So, I heard Jace is taking you for a plane ride this weekend."

"Yeah, I'm excited."

"He's a good guy."

"I know." I can't help but smile.

"Well, you're on your own until ten p.m. Then Elton will relieve you and work overnight," Isaac says as he places his gun in the vault.

"Am I the only female who works security?" I ask.

"Yep. And you're the only girl I know who can shoot a moving object, and has the guts to tackle a criminal," he adds with a smile.

I blush. "I don't understand why everyone keeps making a big deal out of this. Did they even find the other guy who broke in?" I ask.

"No, the car was stolen, and he was wearing gloves, so there weren't any fingerprints."

"They couldn't get Vander to talk?"

"He didn't know anything. The office staff will stay until four thirty or five p.m., and then it will just be you, Giselle, and Hunter, who is interning with Reagan. He will help the dinner volunteer group," he explains.

"Okay, thanks for the tour," I reply.

"No problem. See you tomorrow?"

I shake my head.

"Monday it is, then," he says with a wink and heads toward the door. I sit down at one of the chairs and study the screens. This location is such a similar setup, but I haven't been in security for that long. I need to take in my surroundings before I really feel comfortable. My shift goes by uneventfully.

Chapter 14

I walk out the front door of Grandma's house. Jace is leaning up against his Jeep Wrangler waiting for me. "I was afraid you were going to back out on me," he says as I approach. He is wearing a navy blue shirt, which brings out his eyes.

"And miss the opportunity to see the sunset from the sky?" I reply. "No way." We get into his Jeep, and he puts on a pair of aviator sunglasses. Then he reaches into his glove box and pulls out a women's pair.

"What kind of copilot would you be if you didn't have a pair?" he jokes, handing them to me.

"Thanks," I say as I put them on. I pull down the visor to see how they look in the mirror. "Well, they definitely look better on you than they do on me," I say, and turn so he can see them on my face.

"What are you talking about? You can definitely pull them off. They look good," he replies with a smile.

I look back in the mirror. I guess they look alright on me. They wouldn't be my first choice of sunglasses, but it's sweet that he got them for me.

The drive to the airport takes about forty-five minutes. Jace checks in at the front desk, and we head outside. I have never been on the grounds of an airport before, other than from inside a commercial plane. It's huge. We get into a golf cart and drive over to a smaller plane. "Are you nervous?" he asks.

"A little. I've been on a plane a few times before, but never in the cockpit with the pilot, looking out the front window," I reply.

"Where have you flown to before?" he asks as we get into the plane.

"Florida and Arizona."

"Arizona is beautiful to fly over."

"I can imagine," I say. We climb into the front seats. The seats are closer to each other than I thought they would be. The dashboard looks like a giant collection of knobs, levers, switches, and gauges. I don't know how he remembers what each is for. He pushes a few buttons, then pulls a lever, and we begin to roll onto the runway. Then Jace puts on a headset. Suddenly I am very nervous. "I have nine years' experience flying a plane," he says as if he can sense my anxiety. That doesn't calm me down, though. We make a turn, and he positions the plane in the center of the runway.

"Plane number seven-nine-three-eight-six-three is in position for departure on runway four," he says into the microphone on the headset. He must have gotten the okay to take off, because after a minute we begin to move forward down the runway. He advances the throttle and we accelerate rapidly. My knuckles are clenching the edges of the armrests. What did I get myself into? After a few moments, the plane lifts off the ground, and we begin to ascend.

"Are you okay?" Jace asks as he looks over at me.

I exhale. I didn't even realize I was holding my breath. "Yes," I manage to say, as the plane keeps climbing farther into the sky.

"I guess it's a bit too late to ask if you are afraid of heights," he says.

I shake my head back and forth. "I'm not." I'm glad I'm wearing sunglasses. Hopefully he can't see from the side that my eyes are tightly shut.

After what seems like forever, we finally reach cruising altitude and level out. I take another deep breath. The glass window of the plane doesn't even seem like it's there, it's so clear. We fly into a cloud and everything goes white for a few seconds. Then the sky opens up again. "That was so cool," I say a little too excitedly.

Jace laughs. "I like flying through clouds, too," he says with a grin. "I love seeing how people react to their first plane ride with me." He looks like he is in his element right now. A sense of peace comes over me for the first time since I got on the plane.

"So, how many other girls have you taken up here?" I joke.

He smiles. "I don't invite too many people up here with me. Most of the time I like being up here by myself. It's a good way to clear my head."

I give him a *Yeah, right, you're full of it* look.

He laughs. "I'm serious. I've only brought up a few friends: Isaac, Reagan, and Silas."

I smile. I believe him. "How do you know where you are going?" I ask.

"There is a navigation system, and the traffic controllers can let me know if anything is in my path through reading radar waves," he replies.

I nod my head in understanding.

"We will be over D.C. in a few minutes," he says. Downtown D.C. is filled with large, white historical buildings. It will probably look like a Tetris game of white blocks. "Up ahead are the Appalachian Mountains." He points to the right. The mountain range looks like green waves in the ocean.

"It's beautiful," I say in amazement. This could actually be a really romantic date. Now I am wishing I hadn't reacted the way I did when Jace mentioned the word *date* after inviting me for a plane ride. I gave him the impression that I wasn't interested in him, but now I would like to give it a shot. I'm not sure if the shelter has a policy against employer-employee romantic relationships. Jace is technically my supervisor, so I hope things don't get weird at work if we do start dating.

"How's your grandma handling the chemo?" he asks.

"So far, so good. The first round is usually the easiest," I answer.

"I can't imagine what it would be like to go through that," he comments, staring off into the distance as if in deep thought.

"It's the worst." I pause for a moment. "I had lymphoma when I was in high school."

"Really?" he asks, looking at me. I nod and point to the scar on the middle of my left thigh. "This is where the cancer actually was. This scar is from a biopsy they did before my diagnosis. This scar is from a port," I say, pulling back the neckline on my shirt so he can see that scar, too.

"What's it like...having cancer?" he asks gently.

"Well, when I first found out, I was a little nervous, but I kept a really positive attitude and planned on fighting to the best of my ability. We caught it early, and lymphoma is very curable if found early. I experienced a lot of side effects of chemotherapy, though."

"What kind of side effects?"

I haven't talked about my cancer experience to anyone in a while, but somehow I don't mind right now. "To me chemotherapy felt like poison. It killed the tumor like it was supposed to, but I also lost my hair, I was very tired all the time, and I had terrible body aches and soreness, mouth sores, headaches, and a whole bunch more problems," I explain.

"That sounds horrible. I'm sorry you had to experience that," he says with sincerity.

"Don't get me wrong, it was the most difficult thing I have ever experienced, but I'm a stronger person because of it. I had a lot of support from my family and friends. Their encouragement really helped me. That's why it's so important for me to be there for my grandma," I say.

"Well, I'm willing to help as much as I can, even if it's just being there to support you at a doctor's visit," he says. It's really nice of him to offer help.

"You have already been a huge help. I really appreciate it," I say genuinely.

The sun is setting over the horizon. Pink, orange, and yellow colors paint the sky and tint the clouds. "It's gorgeous," I say. We sit in silence for a few minutes admiring the sunset.

"Ready to head back?" he asks. I nod. Twenty minutes later we are beginning our descent. I think I'd rather sit in the front of the plane for takeoff one thousand times, than sit in the front during a descent, but to my surprise, the plane lands a lot more smoothly than I anticipated. I kept my eyes open through the whole descent, even though it was a bit scary to watch.

Jace steers the plane back to the hangar, where a couple of guys are waiting for us. There are a few other small planes parked nearby. They all look the same to me. We climb down from the plane and walk back to the Jeep. "That was really fun. Thanks for inviting me," I say.

"Anytime you want to go back up, just let me know," he says. "I love flying."

"Do you think you will ever do it professionally someday?" I ask.

"Eh, I don't know. I have thought about it," he replies.

I can feel my phone vibrate in my pocket; there's a text message. I decide to check on it in case it's from my grandma, but it's from Quin. He has an extra ticket for the game tomorrow. I text him back that I might know someone who will come along, planning to ask Jace.

The drive back home flies by as we blast country music and sing along. Jace pulls up in his driveway, and we both hop out. "Thanks again for the plane ride. It was really cool," I say. I'm not sure if I should hug him, or shake his hand; that would probably be more awkward. Luckily he leans in for a hug. He is a bit taller than me. His warm body presses up against my mine. "Hey, what are your plans for tomorrow night?" I ask as I let go.

"I might hang out with Isaac, but we never made set plans to do anything," he replies.

"Well, I have an extra ticket to the Natives game if you want to come. I'm going with a few of my friends."

"Yeah, I'm in. But only because they are playing the Musketeers," he jokes.

"Good, then it's a date," I say with a smile. "Well, a *group* date," I add.

He grins and nods his head in agreement.

"Good night," I say as I begin to walk toward my grandma's house.

"Good night," he calls back.

My mind is racing during the short walk down the sidewalk and up to the front door. Maybe I shouldn't have called it a group date, because that makes it sound like I wouldn't go on a regular date with him. Or does it sound normal? Excitement fills my mind that he said yes and that I get to spend more time with him. I pull out my keys and look over at his house. He is still standing there. I wave. He waves back, then goes inside.

Chapter 15

I walk downstairs the next morning to what appears to be an empty house. Grandma is nowhere to be found. I hope she didn't drive somewhere on her own. One thing about chemotherapy is that dizziness and fatigue can creep up on you pretty suddenly. I don't like the idea of her driving.

As I finish my breakfast in the kitchen, I hear voices coming from the front porch. I go to the hallway, where I can see Grandma sitting on the front porch in her rocking chair, with Jace standing in front of her. "I think you should be honest about it from the start," Grandma says to him.

He sighs. "It's not like I'm lying."

"But that's important information for her to know," she says.

"I will tell her when the time is right, so please don't say anything," Jace says. I shrink back against the wall, trying to become invisible.

"Okay, let me know when you do," she responds.

"Call me if you need anything," Jace says and then walks down the steps and heads back to his house.

That was bizarre. I walk to the front porch. "Good morning, Grandma," I call out. She jumps a bit as if she didn't expect to see me, then folds down the top corner of a page in her book to hold her spot.

"Good morning," she says in return.

"Was someone out here? I thought I heard voices."

"No, it was just me reading my book," she lies. There is no point in pressing the issue because she is so stubborn she would never tell me what she and Jace were talking about anyway.

She picks up her purse from the small glass table next to her. "I have been waiting for you to wake up because I want to go to the farmers' market," she says as she stands up and starts walking to my car.

"I was just on my way to pick up a few things for a tailgating party tonight."

"Good," she says as she gets into the front seat. "Would you mind putting the top down?" she asks. I unlock the top of the convertible, and she holds the button down for it to roll back.

The drive to the farmers' market is a short one. I notice Grandma is letting her hair whip around her face in the wind. It may be one of the last times for a while she will actually be able to feel the wind in her hair.

"How do you feel this morning?" I ask.

"So far, so good, but I didn't want to chance driving myself, just in case," she replies. I nod in understanding. She doesn't look tired at all. There were a few times during chemo that I felt perfectly normal in the morning with plenty of energy, and I would drive myself to school, then all of a sudden, by midday I was dizzy and tired, and I had to call for someone to pick me up.

We walk up to the first few booths of the market, passing a candy shop and a small bank. The market is situated in a park, located in the midst of mom-and-pop shops. There are several vendors that set up tables every Saturday morning during the summer. Some sell freshly baked, homemade pies, and some sell fruits and vegetables from their gardens or farms. Still others sell lawn decorations that they have made by hand, along with other knickknacks. I enjoy browsing through the items and picking out some fresh vegetables. Apparently Grandma enjoys it, too, because she is filling up a basket with more green vegetables than we can possibly eat in one week. "What are you going to do with all that?" I ask her as I examine a cucumber to make sure it's firm enough.

"Juice them," she responds, as she picks through fresh herb bundles.

It sounds odd to be making juice from a stack of carrots, celery, cucumbers, and herbs. "I read about how juicing vegetables is really good for your immune system, and your overall health, so I'm going to try it," she adds. I can't imagine what vegetable juice would taste like. Sounds gross.

While she pays the vendor for her vegetables, I notice that at the end of the tables is a trailer filled with watermelons. That would be great to take to the game tonight. I purchase one, and we walk back to the car. I am glad that Grandma hasn't started losing her strength yet. She seems to be carrying the two bags of vegetables and herbs with ease.

At the grocery store I buy hot dog and hamburger buns, and Grandma picks out a few apples to sweeten up her vegetable juice.

When we get back to her house, I help her peel and slice the vegetables for the week. "What time do you leave for the game tonight?" she asks, as I peel some carrots.

"I think around four o'clock. The game starts at seven, and we plan on grilling beforehand in the parking lot," I reply.

"That will be fun. I remember when your dad used to go to Natives games with your grandfather," she reminisces with a soft smile. My grandfather passed away from a heart attack when I was five. It's difficult to remember him, because I was so young when it happened.

"Do you remember when your dad would take you and Ariana to games when you were younger?" she asks.

"Yeah, I remember going to a few games, back in junior high." Memories begin to flood my mind.

After a few moments of silence, Grandma says, "You know, you can invite your friends over anytime you want. I don't mind. There's no reason for you to hang out with me during all your free time."

I smile. "I don't mind hanging out with you."

"Well, I can finish up here, so go get ready for tonight," she says, shooing me away. I look at the clock. I have an hour to get ready. Where did the time go? I did wake up late, and we must have spent more time at the market and grocery store than I thought. I rush upstairs to get ready.

*****

It takes me forever to figure out what to wear, but I finally decide on white shorts, with my red Natives scoop-neck shirt that has the logo on the front, and my white and black gym shoes. I pull my hair up into a high ponytail to complete the sporty look.

Even though I'm not a Musketeers fan, I still think Jace looks attractive in his gray and orange jersey and baseball cap. We talk about baseball during the ride to the stadium. "So I get to meet all your friends on our first real date? This is a little fast for me, but I guess it's too late to back out now," Jace teases, as we pull into a parking spot next to Jocelyn's car.

I laugh. "No pressure. I have only been friends with two of them for the past ten years, so make a good impression!" I joke back.

"Abrielle!" Natalia shouts with a smile. She runs over, and I kiss her right cheek as she kisses my left. "And who is this handsome guy?" she asks, looking at Jace.

"This is Jace." I introduce him to Natalia. She greets him with a kiss on the cheek, too, which seems to surprise him a bit.

Jocelyn runs up and whispers in my ear as she hugs me, "Paolo and I are official!"

"That's so great!" I exclaim. Jocelyn and Paolo do make a cute couple. "Jace, you remember Jocelyn, and this is her *boyfriend*, Paolo," I say, introducing him next. Paolo holds out his hand.

"I knew there was a reason I didn't like you," Quin says sarcastically to Jace as he walks up. He is wearing his favorite Natives hat and jersey.

"Well, I normally wouldn't set foot in a Natives stadium, if that makes you feel any better, but I had a good reason to come," Jace says, looking at me. I smile back at him.

"Hi, Gabi," I say. She is standing next to Quin holding his hand. 'Hi," she replies with what seems to be a forced smile. I wonder if something is bothering her. She was really outgoing the other two times we hung out.

We begin to set up the grill and fill a table with snacks. Paolo sets up some chairs, and Jace brings out the cooler we brought. I pull out the reusable water bottles I had filled with a homemade cranberry punch, and take a sip.

"What's that?" Quin asks. I offer him the bottle and he takes a sip. "It's good, but it would be better with vodka," he replies sarcastically.

I roll my eyes. "What is it with you and alcohol lately?" I ask. He shrugs his shoulders. It seems like every time we hang out, he is drinking, even getting drunk.

"I think it's perfect just the way it is," Jace says softly as he wraps his arm around my waist with his free hand, the bottle I made for him in his other hand.

"Thanks," I say. His touch is soothing.

"Oh, we need to take pictures before some people get past the point of looking normal in a picture," Jocelyn exclaims as she looks pointedly at Quin. She whips out her phone, and Jace pulls me in closer to him. I think I could get used to this. She snaps a picture of us, then of Quin and Gabi, then I take one of her and Paolo.

We ask the group of guys tailgating next to us to take a group pic. Jace is on my right with his arm around my waist, and Quin is on my left with his arm around my shoulder. It's a little awkward. For so long I had wondered if it could ever work out with Quin, but suddenly I wish I were alone with Jace. Jace has the courage to act on his feelings, and I find his confidence attractive. The guy takes the picture, and we all spread out again. It's another warm summer evening.

"Alright, let's get this grill started," Quin says as he starts to unbutton his jersey.

"What are you doing?" Gabi asks.

"Taking my jersey off so I don't get grease on it," he replies. He is wearing a form-fitting white T-shirt underneath. The bottom half of his tattoo is clearly visible.

"Whoa! When did you get that?" Jocelyn asks, pointing to his tattoo as she walks over to look at it more closely. I didn't tell her about it, because I didn't want to talk about it.

"A couple of days ago," he answers. Gabi purses her lips. Natalia rushes over to look at it, too.

"What does it stand for?" Natalia asks, not knowing my history. Quin looks at me, and I hold his gaze for a few moments, then look away. I can feel myself starting to blush.

"I have a really good friend who battled cancer," he replies. Gabi looks agitated. I wonder if she is mad about the tattoo. I would be if I were her. "The boxing gloves represent the fight. Very clever," Paolo chimes in.

Jace looks at the tattoo, then at me. "Is that about you?" he leans in and whispers, apparently not wanting it to seem strange if he is wrong. His breath is warm against my ear and sends goose bumps down my arm. I nod my head. This is uncomfortable. Everyone is gathered around Quin making comments about his new tat. Gabi looks to be getting angrier by the second, and finally she storms off. Quin rolls his eyes and doesn't even try to go after her. His body language tells me that they have had an argument over his tattoo before.

For some reason I feel compelled to chase after her, as if this is all my fault. "I'll be right back," I say to Jace. "Gabi, wait up!" I call after her. She is a few car lengths ahead, weaving in and out of groups of people. I quickly catch up because my legs are longer than hers. "Gabi, wait," I call again.

"Leave me alone," she retorts as she continues to walk. We finally get to a clearing in between aisles of cars, and I run to get in front of her. She stops, and it looks like she is trying to hold back tears. "Are you and Quin…hooking up?" she asks angrily.

"No, we have never been together," I say. She doesn't need to know that he was my first kiss, because nothing else happened after that. She rolls her eyes.

"He doesn't look at me the way he looks at you," she complains.

I have never noticed him looking at me differently from any other girl. "Look, we grew up together, and he was there for me when my mom died from cancer, and during my own battle. It really impacted him. That's why he got the tattoo. And if there's one thing I'm sure of, it's that he would never cheat on anyone," I respond.

She sniffles. "Okay, you're probably right. I think I'm just a little jealous. It's not like I would want him to get a tattoo for me, though. We have only been dating, like, six weeks."

I nod. On the one hand I understand her jealousy, but on the other hand, it brings out a different side of her, which makes it difficult to understand why he would stay with her.

"Let's head back," I say gently.

"How am I supposed to go back over there after I stormed off like that? It will be so awkward."

"Just say you had to go to the bathroom."

She nods. "Good idea." We start to head back. Part of me wishes I had let her storm off. Quin doesn't need another overly jealous girlfriend.

"This is my first Natives game."

"Well, you're in for a treat, because they are going to win today!" I say with confidence. When we walk back up to the group, Jocelyn is sitting on Paolo's lap, and they seem oblivious to the world, Quin is grilling, and Jace is talking to Natalia. Gabi opens a beer and stands over by Quin.

"Is everything okay?" Jace asks genuinely. I nod my head. I notice that Quin and Gabi are talking, but I can't hear what they are saying. He stretches his arm out to grab her waist, pulls her close to him, and they kiss.

"Natalia, how are your summer classes going?" I ask, trying to cover up the fact that I was just staring at Quin and Gabi.

"They are great. I'm taking a class about illegal immigrants and my second semester of Aramaic," she replies.

"That's really interesting. What's your major?" Jace asks.

"I'm in law school. I originally wanted to work for a big corporation, but after living in the States for the past two years, I'm switching my concentration to focus on helping immigrants," she replies.

"That's really cool. I have a friend who could use an immigration lawyer," Jace states. I wonder if he is referring to a client at the shelter.

"Well, I'm not a lawyer yet, but I might be able to help a little bit," Natalia offers.

"Food is ready," Quin shouts. Everyone fills a plate with food and finds a chair. I love summer days like this when I can hang out with my friends, grill, and enjoy the weather. My cell phone begins to vibrate in my pocket, interrupting my blissful moment. I pull it out, just to make sure it's not my grandma. It's a number I don't recognize. Normally I let those calls go to voice mail, but for some reason I feel compelled to answer it.

"Hello?" I speak into the phone as I stand up.

"Hi, is this Abrielle Peregrine?" a polite voice asks from the other end.

"Yes, who is this?" I ask, thinking it might be a telemarketer. I walk away from the group.

"This is a nurse from the ER at North Beach Hospital. We have your grandmother here for some testing. She has been coughing up blood for the past two hours, and she's complained of dizziness and trouble breathing," the nurse reports.

"Oh my gosh! How did she get to the hospital?" I ask, as I try not to panic.

"She called an ambulance for herself. You are listed as the emergency contact in our records," the nurse responds.

"Okay. I will be there as soon as I can, thank you."

I hang up and stand there for a moment in shock, hoping that Grandma is okay. She seemed perfectly fine earlier. Jace is walking toward me. "Is everything okay?" he asks, as he gets closer to me.

"My grandma is in the emergency room."

He looks worried, but replies calmly, "I'll take you there." We quickly move things out of the way so he can back the Jeep out.

"Text me later so I know she's okay," Quin says.

"Yeah, let us know how she is as soon as you find out." Jocelyn hugs me.

"I will," I respond. We quickly say good-bye to everyone and get into the Jeep. It takes a little while to get out of the parking lot because people are still tailgating. We get a few glares from people who are forced to move their party aside so that we can get through. If only they knew I was on my way to the hospital. I text my sister and dad to let them know what happened. A million thoughts are racing through my mind. Why didn't Grandma call me herself? Is she going to be okay?

"I'm sure she is going to be fine," Jace says soothingly, as if he can read my mind. He reaches for my hand. His touch is calming. I nod my head, hoping he is right.

Chapter 16

Jace and I walk in through the front door of my grandma's house. "I feel bad just leaving her there at the hospital alone," I say as I set my house keys down on the table. Jace has just spent the past three hours at the hospital with me. Grandma is hooked up to oxygen, and the doctor said the test results would be back in the morning. They want to monitor her overnight.

"You will get a better night's sleep in your own bed, though. You will need all the energy you can get to be able to take care of her tomorrow when they release her," he responds.

"I know. You're right." Although I have the feeling I might just toss and turn all night in worry no matter where I am.

"I'm sorry I ruined your night," I say as I search his eyes to try and gauge his disappointment.

"My night was not ruined." He takes a step closer to me. "I still got to spend it with you." He brushes a piece of hair away from my face.

"Well, I still want to make it up to you somehow. Like, a real date, just the two of us," I respond as I gently wrap my arms around his neck. He leans in, and his lips press against mine. They are soft and seem to fit perfectly against my mouth. He pulls back long enough to whisper, "Deal," then leans back in, resting his hands on my hips. For a moment, I forget everything that has happened today and lose myself in his embrace.

*****

"Bri!" my sister shouts from the bottom of the stairs. I bolt upright in bed. *What time is it?* I think frantically. I need to pick up Grandma from the hospital. The sun is streaming through my window. I grab my phone to check the time, but it's dead. I must have forgotten to charge it last night. I can hear Dad's voice downstairs, and Ariana's feet pounding on the stairs as she runs up to my room. I plug my phone in to its charger by the nightstand. "Oh, good, you are alive," my sister says sarcastically as she comes in the door.

"What time is it?" I ask.

"Almost noon," she replies.

"Seriously?" I ask in shock. I never sleep in that late.

"Yeah, Dad and I went straight to the hospital this morning, and they released Grandma so we brought her home. I called you a couple of times, but—"

"My phone died," I cut her off.

"But you were too busy dreaming about Jace," she finishes in a singsong voice. I can't help but smile when she says his name.

"Oh my gosh, you kissed him! Tell me everything!" she says, grinning.

My attempt not to get excited at her remark fails, and my smile only grows bigger. "I really like him. He's genuine, and sweet, and I can't wait to see him again. I just hope things don't get weird at work," I respond.

"You both work with his mom. I don't think it gets any weirder than that," she says with a snicker.

"Right. Well, I'm going to take a quick shower, and then I'll come downstairs."

Fifteen minutes later, I walk into the living room. Grandma is sitting in her favorite chair, and my dad and sister are on the couch next to her. Grandma looks weak and tired. I hate to see her like this. As positive as she is, I am starting to have a hard time believing she can overcome this battle, given her age. I try not to think about it.

"The doctor said Grandma isn't responding well to the chemo they're using right now, so they are going to try a different kind in a few days," Dad says, waving a small stack of papers from the hospital.

"Sorry I didn't come to pick you up this morning," I say to Grandma. I sit down on the couch next to her and put my hand on top of hers.

"It's okay," she says softly.

"I wish you would have called me yesterday as soon as you started experiencing symptoms."

"I didn't want to bother you. I felt okay at first, and then all of a sudden I was so dizzy. I think I'm going to take a nap."

Ariana stands up to help Grandma to her room.

Once they are out of earshot, Dad says, "It's so hard to see her like this."

I nod my head in agreement. "I just wish she would ask for help more. What's the point of me living here if she's not going to let me help her?"

Dad shrugs his shoulders and shakes his head. "Well, what needs to be done around here?" he asks.

"I was going to clean the house today."

"Alright. Ariana can help with that. The grass needs to be cut, so I'll be outside." He kisses my forehead, then walks toward the back door.

*****

I arrive at the shelter about thirty minutes before the office opens. There are four other vehicles in the parking lot: Jace's and three cars I don't recognize yet. I just couldn't sleep with so many concerns about my grandma's health occupying my mind. My body was too tired to go for a run, but I figured I could get some things done for the charity ball before my shift starts. I walk into the front reception area. The sunshine streams through the front glass doors and lights up the hallway.

When I open the door to the offices, I see Isaac sitting at Tia's desk. He is sitting across from a man in a gray suit. I can't hear what they are saying from across the room, though. Whatever they were talking about it looks like they are done. They both stand up and shake hands. Jace comes out of Dalilah's office. He looks surprised to see me. The man in the suit opens his jacket as he walks past me to put his notepad away. There is a Homeland Security Badge clipped to his inner pocket.

"Good morning," Isaac and Jace say in unison.

"You're early," Jace says with a forced smile.

"Why was Homeland Security here?" I ask. They both look surprised.

"He just had some questions about some of the clients who come here," Isaac answers. He stares at the floor as he speaks. I don't believe him.

"Kind of weird that he would want to talk to you and not the case worker."

Jace looks uncomfortable. "He was here because of me. When we moved to the States, my parents had no trouble becoming legal. But my paperwork just went through."

It still doesn't make sense. Wouldn't Homeland Security have interviewed people about Jace *before* they approved his paperwork, not after? There's something they're not telling me, but I don't feel like playing detective this morning. Considering the fact that Jace didn't let Isaac lie to me, I assume he will come around eventually and tell me the whole truth. I go over to my workstation and grab my security belt and lanyard.

When I turn around, Jace and Isaac are silently gesturing at each other and mouthing words. They stop when they see me. "Do you want me to leave?" I ask, suspicious.

"No. I'm sorry I'm being weird this morning. I'm going to make a donut run for the staff. Do you want a coffee?" Jace replies. We have a coffee machine here, but the place down the street is way better.

"Yeah, an iced coffee would be great." He comes over and kisses me on the cheek before he leaves.

"So I take it the plane ride went well, then?" Isaac asks playfully.

I smile. "Yeah, it did."

*****

"Hey, will you walk me to my car?" I ask Jace at the end of my shift. He smiles and nods. Part of me wants to question him more about this morning. We aren't even dating, though, so is it really my business? I just don't want this to be a relationship in which we hide things from each other.

As we walk to my car, I notice the purple Challenger again. I had thought it was Dalilah's car, but she's not here today.

"Okay, I can tell there's something on your mind, so what is it?"

I hesitate. "I just feel like there's something you're not telling me."

He looks into my eyes for a moment before responding. "Even though I'm a legal citizen now, I'm scared they are going to say, 'Sorry, we made a mistake,' and ship me back to South Africa."

I smile sympathetically. I wasn't expecting him to say that. "That can't happen," I say as I take his hand.

"Good, because there's this girl that I really want to spend more time with," he says with a grin. I wrap my arms around him and hug him good-bye. Then he kisses me, and it erases any doubts I've had about him. "Thank you for being honest with me," I say before I get into my car.

Chapter 17

The next day, Grandma and I are waiting at the hospital for the nurse to start her on a new type of chemo. This type is supposed to be more aggressive than the last, which means stronger side effects. I really hate sitting around in infusion rooms, but I am glad I can be there for her. There is a knock on the already open door. "Hello!" Felicity says cheerfully from the doorway as she holds her intravenous stand for support.

"Hi, Felicity! What's new?" I ask.

"Same old stuff," she replies. Her jacket hangs off her left shoulder, and the IV line dangles from her port. She pulls a scarf out of her pocket.

"Faustina, are you going to wear a wig or scarves?" she asks as she plays with the scarf in her hand.

"I will probably were a scarf like Abrielle did," she says.

Felicity looks like she is deep in thought. "You weren't worried that people would know something was wrong with you?" she asks me.

I smile. "I felt even more self-conscious wearing a wig. The scarves were fun to wear, even though a lot of people stared."

She runs her fingers over the scarf in her hand. "Can you show me how to tie this? I have been thinking about wearing it, but I'm not sure."

"Sure. Have a seat," I say. I take my handheld mirror out of my purse and hand it to her so she can watch. She takes her wig off and puts it on her lap. I feel honored that she is comfortable enough around me to take her wig off. I never wanted anyone to see me without something on my head. I stand behind her and fold the scarf in half. Then I place it on her head, tying it to the side with an elastic band, as if I am fixing her hair into a low bun. She is watching intently.

"This looks awesome!" she exclaims excitedly.

"There you are!" Vivian cries out from the doorway. "I was looking all over for you!" She stops for a second when she sees her daughter in the scarf. She looks like she might cry.

"What do you think?" Felicity asks enthusiastically.

"I think everyone will know you have cancer if you don't wear your wig." Vivian purses her lip.

"Everyone already knows, Mom," she says, clearly upset as she stands up.

"Let's go back to your station. You shouldn't be wandering around out here," Vivian says. She grabs the wig and steers her daughter out of the room.

"You should be her mentor," Grandma says when they're out of earshot.

"Who knows if she even wants a mentor?" I ask.

"Seems to me like she could use some support."

I sit back down. The nurse comes in and hooks up the first bag of chemo.

"Now, I don't want you to be mad at me, but I know between helping me and working, you haven't had much time to see your friends. I feel terrible that you missed the baseball game last weekend, too, so I invited some of your friends over for a cookout tonight," she says.

I am both grateful and caught off guard at the same time. "Grandma, I appreciate it, but it's a weeknight, so I doubt they will be able to drive out, plus you need to rest," I say.

"I can rest when I'm dead. Plus, they are probably already on their way. Ariana went out to buy food, and they will most likely be at the house by the time you get back," she says with a smile. She has to stay in the hospital overnight the first few days during this new chemo.

"I wasn't planning on leaving you here alone," I say.

"I'm not alone, the nurses will be here," she insists. I sigh.

I could use a night with my friends to help take my mind off things. I spent the rest of yesterday and this morning helping Grandma sort through things in her second guest bedroom, and I haven't seen Jace in two days. The job we did was more like me going through her boxes as she lay on the couch, drifting to sleep and occasionally coming back to and making comments about what to donate or throw out. I wonder who she invited over.

* * * * *

Quin is flipping burgers and chicken on the grill, while Jocelyn, Ariana, Isaac, and Reagan sit around the patio table talking. "Sorry I haven't called you since your shift ended yesterday," Jace says, as I gaze out the kitchen window at my friends and fix the potato salad.

"It's okay. I know you are busy with work." Both he and Dalilah seem to always be working. I suppose there is a lot more to do when you are in charge of two locations. I grab the potato salad and some paper plates, while he grabs utensils and chips and we head outside.

"Hey, you haven't given me a recent update about your grandma, or how you're doing," Quin says quietly as I am about to walk past him.

I shrug. "I've been busy."

"It worries me when I don't hear that you are both okay," Quin says in a low voice.

"Shouldn't you be worrying about your girlfriend instead of me?" I ask. I don't know why he is acting like I need to check in with him. I texted him the day my grandma came home, and I haven't talked to him since.

"We broke up."

"Oh," I say. I notice Jace staring at us from the patio table. I'm sure he is wondering what we are whispering about, so I walk over to the table and set down the potato salad and plates. I don't know how else to respond to Quin's breakup anyway. I wasn't a fan of Gabi in the first place, but that was because I wanted to date Quin. Now that I have moved on, it doesn't matter to me who he dates. But I still wonder why they broke up.

"Paolo and Natalia both wanted to come tonight but they had to work," Jocelyn says, interrupting my thoughts.

"I'm actually surprised all of you were able to make it on such short notice." I'm glad Ariana has arranged this, but the fact that I'm not with my grandma at the hospital worries me a bit.

"I didn't have anything else going on," Jocelyn says before she takes a sip of water.

Reagan is acting strange. She keeps making inside jokes, which only seem to be understood by her, Jace, and Isaac. She and Isaac laugh, but Jace seems to be uncomfortable.

"What have you been up to the past few days?" I ask Jace as I rest my hand on his leg. We have been texting a bit, but my focus has been on my grandma.

"Working overtime at the shelter. There's been a lot going on at the D.C. location. I'm glad I can take a break from it all to see you, though." He puts his hand on top of mine.

"Food is done," Quin announces before he takes a sip of his beer. It's really tempting to join Quin and Isaac for a drink, to relieve some of the stress I have been under, but I decide not to.

I lean over toward Ariana. "You can stay with Grandma tomorrow, right?" I have to work all day.

"Yeah, I was planning on it," she replies as she grabs some chips.

I breathe a sigh of relief.

"Bri, don't worry. I've got it covered. The point of this night was for you to take your mind *off* of Grandma."

"I know, but I can't help it."

"Well, she would want you to try." She grabs her plate. "I'm going inside, where it's a little quieter," she says as she stares at Reagan.

"So, Bri, how do you like it at the other shelter?" Quin asks while opening another beer.

I shrug a shoulder. "It's good. I like working in security." It's nice to have a break from all the details and organization that is needed as the volunteer coordinator.

My favorite song comes on the radio, and I lean back in my chair. We all sit around and talk, just enjoying the weather and each other's company for hours. Reagan has been flirting with Quin all night. I'm surprised he's not flirting back, especially since he has been drinking. When Quin doesn't respond to her, Reagan finally turns to Isaac. He responds to her flirtatious comments, but his attention doesn't seem to satisfy her.

I try to catch Jace's attention. When our eyes meet, he says, "I have to take care of something at the shelter. I'll call you tomorrow." Then he kisses my cheek. I admire his dedication to work, but I am also curious to know what is so urgent at ten o'clock at night that he needs to leave our get-together. He and Isaac take off. Reagan looks disappointed when they leave.

"I think I'm going to head home, too. I have to work in the morning," Jocelyn says.

"Alright, thanks for driving out," I say as I hug her goodbye.

"Are you going to be okay with Drunky McGee over there?" she asks.

I look over at Quin, who is slouched in a lawn chair, looking at his phone, with eight empty beer bottles in front of him. He has been drinking a lot lately. It worries me a little. "Yeah, he can sleep in the other guest room upstairs." I sigh.

"Thanks for having us over," Jocelyn adds.

"It was nice to relax with everyone," I say. Jocelyn leaves, and it's just Reagan, Quin, and me. I haven't talked to Reagan much tonight—not because I didn't want to, but because she seemed too wrapped up in the guys.

"We can hang out a little longer if you don't have to be anywhere tomorrow," I suggest.

"No, I'd better get going." She walks over and stands with her arms folded in front of me. "So, you and Jace are dating?"

"Well, we have been hanging out, but he's not my boyfriend or anything."

She lowers her voice so Quin can't hear. "I have seen a lot of girls throw themselves at him for his money. I hope you're not one of them." She sounds like she cares about him a lot. I wonder how long they have been friends.

"That doesn't matter to me," I say, confused. She looks me up and down, as if trying to determine whether or not I am telling the truth.

"Okay. Have a good night," she finally says, then walks past me.

"You, too," I say hesitantly. That was weird. She leaves, and I walk over to Quin, taking the half-empty beer bottle out of his hand. "C'mon, it's time for bed," I say. He sticks his arm out for me to help him up. I grab his hand and pull. He jumps out of the chair and lands a little too close to me.

"I'm not as drunk as you think I am, you know," he says as he stares into my eyes. I let go of his hand.

"I'm not as dumb as you think I am," I respond. Surprisingly he walks to the door without stumbling, and we quietly walk inside. Ariana is sleeping on the couch. "You can sleep in the other bedroom upstairs," I say.

We tiptoe upstairs and I point him to the guest bedroom, then go to brush my teeth. When I come out of the bathroom and walk into my room, Quin is standing there by my dresser, wearing only his shorts, looking at the picture of his tattoo that he gave me. I am caught off guard, as I've already put my pajamas on. I clear my throat. He looks at me and smiles. "Did you get lost looking for the bathroom?" I ask.

"No, I just wanted to talk," he replies.

Great, I'm never going to get to bed, I think. "Why did you and Gabi break up?" I ask, thinking he must want to talk about her, as I walk across the room to sit on my bed. He moves away from the dresser and stops me in the middle of the room.

"Because she thinks I'm in love with you," he says softly as he looks straight into my eyes. My heart starts beating faster.

He places his hands on my hips. I can feel my face growing warm.

"Well, that's—" I start to say "that's ridiculous," but he cuts me off.

"I *am* in love with you," he says and leans closer.

My stomach drops. I have wanted to hear those words for so long.

"I always have been," he adds quietly right before he kisses me. His lips are warm, and he tastes like beer. My heart is racing now.

I wrap my arms around his neck, and he pulls me closer. His kiss is everything I remembered it to be and more. I feel like I can't catch my breath. If he is really ready to be in a relationship with me, I suddenly think I am willing to give up anything that might have been with Jace. I pull away for a moment. "I love you, too," I say, our foreheads touching. He smiles and kisses me again. I feel like I'm dreaming, the moment is so perfect. His right hand wraps around my backside, pulling me as he walks backward, guiding me toward my bed. I'm so lost in his kiss, I don't even notice.

"I have...been waiting...for this...forever..." he says in between kisses.

"Me, too."

"Should we close your door?" he asks.

I look at the door, then back at him. My eyes grow wide. I let go of him. "We are *not* having sex, if that's what you think is going to happen," I exclaim.

He looks confused.

"I have been waiting forever to be with you, and all you have been waiting for is to have sex with me?" I ask angrily.

"No, no, it's not like that," he says, trying to pull me closer again. "It's the best way I know how to show you I love you," he adds, as he leans in to kiss me again, but I push him away.

"You show me you love me every time you put on a uniform and put your life on the line. Love is about more than sex, it's about sacrifice."

He sighs. "C'mon, Bri. It's not like we just met yesterday. We have known each other for years," he responds, taking my hands in his.

"I promised my mom before she died that I would wait until marriage. You know she was religious, and I don't fully understand *why* it was important to her, but I made a promise and I'm going to keep it," I say, folding my arms across my chest.

He runs his fingers through his hair. "So, you're saying that if we are together, it will not happen at all?" he asks in disbelief.

I slowly nod my head. "It will be hard, but I think we can make it work."

He is staring off into the corner of my room, shaking his head. "I...I can't do that. Sex is an important part of a relationship to me."

How could I go from feeling like everything was perfect, to feeling so deeply hurt, all within a couple of minutes? "So, we aren't even going to try dating, then?" I ask.

"Not unless you're willing to break a promise that you don't even understand," he says coldly as he stands up.

I am in shock. "Get out of my room," I say sternly. He stares at me for a moment in disbelief, then walks out.

It takes a lot of restraint to quietly close the door. If Ariana weren't here, I would slam it shut. I can't even believe him. I turn my lamp off and lie down. Warm tears roll down my cheeks. If he really loved me, he would have accepted the promise I made to my mom. I don't understand. I try to convince myself that he was just drunk, and he might not have meant what he said. But all I know is if that's how he truly feels, then we can never be together. I don't even know if we can be friends at all anymore. My head is throbbing, and my heart is aching. The fact that he doesn't even want to try to have a relationship with me hurts. I keep replaying the past few minutes in my mind until I finally drift off to sleep.

*****

The smell of bacon and hash browns wafts up to my room. I roll out of bed and throw some clothes on. When I walk into the kitchen, Quin has a breakfast buffet set up, complete with fresh-squeezed orange juice. "Why are you still here?" I ask coldly as I cross my arms. I thought for sure he would have been gone by the time I woke up.

"Ummm, I'm making breakfast for you and your sister?" he offers.

"Quin, after what happened last night, I don't think we should hang out for a while. I would like you to leave," I say bitterly.

Quin rushes over to me. "Bri, I don't remember anything that happened. I was drunk," he says. I search his eyes. "The last thing I remember was walking upstairs," he adds. He looks desperate. His words sting. The fact that he told me he loved me, and now he doesn't even remember, hurts almost as much as the fact that all he wanted to do was sleep with me. I try to fight back tears.

"Your eyes are puffy. Were you crying?" he asks as he gently touches the side of my face.

I swat his hand away.

"Bri, what did I do?" he asks sincerely.

I shake my head and wipe a tear from my eye. Part of me wants to tell him what happened, but the other part of me wonders if what he said was just the alcohol talking. "I don't ever want to talk about it," I say.

He wraps his arms around me. "Whatever I did or said last night, I'm sorry. I never meant to hurt you," he responds.

His hug is bittersweet. I don't hug him back, so he lets go.

Even though he doesn't seem to remember, I can't look at him the same way anymore. On the one hand, at least I now know that we could never be together. On the other hand, it hurts to be in the same room with him. He lingers in front of me.

"Why have you been drinking so much lately anyway?" Maybe last night would have been different if he hadn't been drunk.

He shrugs his shoulders. "I don't know. I guess...so that I don't have to deal with stuff."

"That's stupid. Whatever you're trying to put off will still be there when you sober up." I can feel my forehead crease as I speak.

"Fair enough. I guess I should be honest with you then..." He squeezes his eyes shut and takes a deep breath. "I..." he pauses and looks to the ground. "I do remember everything that happened last night, and I'm sorry for the way I acted. When I saw how upset you were, I thought for a minute it might be better to pretend like I didn't know." His eyes meet mine. He looks desperate.

This time I am the one to look away. His words pierce my heart, and all the emotions I felt last night flood my mind again. My mouth opens as if to say something, but I don't know what to say in response. He has never lied to me before. I want to scream at him for being a jerk, ask him if he meant what he said last night, demand to know why he thought it was a good idea to lie. None of these things come out, though.

I take a deep breath. "I need some space. Please don't call me or text me." I walk around him and sit at the kitchen table.

"Bri—"

"Please. Just leave," I say, putting my hand up to stop him from talking. My other hand closes tightly around the fork he has set out for me.

He doesn't say anything back. I reach for the hash browns. He stands there for a moment, sighs, and then walks out. I fill my plate, but suddenly I'm not hungry. I need to go for a run to clear my mind. I put my sneakers on, stretch for a few minutes, and start out with a light jog. The sun warms my skin.

I jog past Jace's house. His Jeep isn't there. He's probably at work. What will he think about all of this? It's not like he has officially asked me to be his girlfriend, so technically I didn't cheat on him. Part of me feels like I did, though. I can't stop replaying last night in mind, like it's a puzzle and I'm trying to figure out if I did something wrong to make it to turn out the way it did.

I think about how Quin treated me differently at the beginning of the summer, how it felt like we were dating, but we hadn't kissed. I think about his tattoo, and everything we have been through together. How can he tell me he loves me, and then just decide not to give it a try based on one thing? I try to convince myself that since he cared so much about sex, he would just be using me. Given our history and friendship,

I feel that we have bonded on so many different levels, though, and I can't imagine ever feeling the same connection with anyone else. Maybe that's why I can't stop thinking about him.

Maybe it hurts so much because I love him, and because I wanted to be with him for so long. After all these years of waiting for the right moment, of pushing my feelings for him aside, I finally got my answer. We would never work out. It's hard to accept, but at least now I can move on without regrets of what could have been.

Jace is a really great guy. I need to tell him what happened last night, even if it means losing him. It's going to be hard. But I don't want him to find out from someone else later on in our relationship. I hope he's at the shelter early so I can talk to him. The mistake I made with Quin is that we never told each other before how we felt. Maybe things would have turned out differently if we had just been honest with each other sooner.

Chapter 18

I walk into the D.C. shelter with Jocelyn. We talked on the phone while I drove to work. I feel much better after talking to her about what happened. I needed to tell someone, and to figure out the best way to tell Jace. We head toward the meeting room. Isaac is already in there, writing something in his notebook. "Hey, ladies, how's it going?" he asks.

"Good, how about you?" I answer.

"I'm good, but I don't know about your boyfriend." He nods his head toward Jace, who has quietly walked in behind me. I blush. I am not sure how to respond to his comment about Jace being my boyfriend. It's even more awkward since he is standing right there. Unlike Quin, though, he doesn't deny being my boyfriend. That makes me happy inside.

"Hey, can we go somewhere else and talk?" Jace asks me.

"Yeah," I reply. I begin to worry. What does he want to talk about? There is no way he could know about what happened between me and Quin last night, I assure myself. We walk out of the room, and Jace unlocks the smaller counseling office, then closes the door behind us. Neither of us sits down.

"I saw Quin's truck outside of your grandma's house this morning when I left for work, and I can't help but wonder if something happened between you two. There's the whole tattoo thing and—" Jace moves his hands around a lot when he talks.

"I wanted to talk to you about that," I interrupt him.

His shoulders drop a bit, as if every negative thought that entertained his mind about Quin and me is true. "Abrielle, I see the way he looks at you, and I know you two have been friends for a while. If there is something going on between you, I don't want to get in the middle of it. I really like you, but I don't want to be the *other* guy," he responds as he searches my eyes.

I take a step toward him. "Jace, I want to be with you," I say with more confidence than I feel at the moment.

He sighs in relief. "I was really hoping you would say that," he responds as he comes closer and leans in to kiss me.

"I need to be honest with you, though, about what happened last night," I say, stopping him. He hesitates and looks a little surprised.

"Okay, what happened?"

"Last night Quin and I kissed."

Jace sighs. "Well, since we never determined what our relationship would be, I can't be mad. A little jealous, maybe," he says as his mouth forms a half smile. He pauses for a moment as if in thought, then says, "You guys have a long history, so how can I trust that this isn't going to happen again?" he asks.

I swallow hard. I don't want to tell him about our fight over sex. What if he reacts the same way? What if he thinks I'm weird? What if he doesn't believe me? I take a deep breath and decide to take the plunge. "I feel like if you and I are going to make our relationship work, then we need to be honest with each other."

"Okay. Yeah, I agree," he says as he looks at the ground, a hint of worry mixed with curiosity in his voice.

"Last night Quin was pressuring me to have sex with him. I said no. I am sure that I can never be with him because I promised my mom before she died I would wait until marriage to have sex. It was really important to her, and so it's really important to me. Quin basically said he couldn't be with someone who wouldn't have sex with him."

Jace doesn't respond, so I stare at the floor. He must think I'm crazy. He probably wants to end it with me right now for telling him that. I hope telling him the whole story doesn't mean I will lose him, but at least I didn't keep anything from him.

"I'm so sorry you had to experience that last night," he finally says, to my surprise. He wraps his arms around me and hugs me tightly. His touch is calming, and I'm taken aback by his understanding. "I just want you to know that part of me wants to kick his ass for pressuring you to do something you didn't want to do. I would never do that to you."

I pull back a little from his hug, still wrapped in his arms. "Well, I won't be hanging out with him much anymore, especially since I have the most amazing, understanding boyfriend of all times," I say with a smile.

He smiles back, and we kiss, slow, soft, and gentle. It's a relief to hear him say he won't pressure me to go further than I'm willing to go.

After a moment, he pulls back. "I *really* want this to work, Abrielle, but a little part of me feels like I'm your second choice. I mean, you told Quin no because of a promise you made to your mom, not because of me," he says sincerely and searches my eyes.

I can sense the hurt in his voice. I hadn't thought of it that way. He's right, though. I look deeply into his eyes, then reply in complete honesty, "Jace, you are the most sincere, genuine, thoughtful, understanding guy I have ever met. You have this way of making me feel like I am the only person in the room when you talk to me..." He smiles, and I go on. "And you are ridiculously good-looking, too, so that's a plus." I try to lighten the mood.

"I believe you." He smiles.

I'm so glad he isn't mad about what happened last night, but I am worried that I need to prove to him that he isn't my second choice. "Since we are being open and honest with each other, there's something I need to ask you about. The other day I heard you talking to my grandma on the front porch, something about a secret. What were you guys talking about?" I ask.

He takes a deep breath and exhales. "How about I tell you over dinner Friday night?"

"I think that could be arranged," I say, smiling stupidly like a love-struck teenage girl.

"As much as I want to stay here and kiss you all day, we should get to the meeting."

"Okay. To be continued," I say.

We walk down the hallway toward the meeting room where everyone is already gathered.

*****

I open the front door of my house. "Hello?" There's no answer. I'm supposed to have dinner with Dad, but he doesn't seem to be home yet. I plop down on the couch and call him. Again, no answer. I sigh and lean back. Sitting in the family room makes me realize how much I miss being home.

A text message pops up from Dad: "Hey, I'm working late again. I should have texted you sooner. Rain check?"

"Sure," I reply.

I get up and walk across the hardwood floor. I know I won't be moving back here anytime soon. I lock the door behind me and walk toward my car. There are a few hours of sunlight left in the day, so maybe I can go for a jog when I get back to Grandma's. I glance to my left and notice Quin sitting on his front steps, looking at his phone. I pick up the pace walking to my car, hoping he doesn't notice me.

I'm too late. "Hey, Bri, wait up," he calls as he jogs down the stairs and over to me. I want to ignore him, but for some reason I stop and wait. "You haven't been answering my calls or texts," he says, sounding truly concerned.

I can feel my eyebrows instantly furrow. "That's because I don't want to talk to you," I say in an annoyed tone.

He looks somewhat shocked. "Are you still mad about the other night?"

I look away angrily, shaking my head. "Quin, I told you, I need space right now." I turn to leave.

Quin races in front of me and stops, blocking the path to my car.

"I can take you out," I say, half-serious, half-joking.

"I know, but I just can't stand it when you're mad at me. I need you in my life, Bri."

He is so full of it. "You should've thought about that before you got drunk and said things you probably didn't mean," I say, stepping around him.

He lets me walk past him. "Bri, I don't know what else to say. I'm sorry."

"You already said everything you need to, Quin." I open my car door.

"So, I guess this is a bad time to tell you I got us two tickets for the Natives game tomorrow night, right behind home plate," he says with hope in his voice. Those are really good tickets. It's tempting go to the game with him, but I'm still mad.

"Jace and I are exclusive now. I don't want to do anything to jeopardize our relationship, and I think hanging out with you as much as I normally do would send him the wrong message," I respond.

He looks defeated. "When did that happen?"

"Today."

He slowly nods his head in understanding, then starts to walk toward his house. It's a little satisfying to see him hurting, after he hurt me so badly.

I get into my car and drive to the hospital.

Chapter 19

The nurse comes in and hooks up the chemo to Grandma's IV. Her hair has started thinning and falling out already. She is wearing it down and loose, pulled over her right shoulder. We will probably need to buzz it off soon. I remember losing my hair. It was almost as devastating as finding out I had cancer. It was a difficult decision to get it shaved off, but it seemed less traumatic to do that than to find clumps of hair around the house.

"How are you feeling today, Faustina?" the nurse asks cheerfully.

"I'm not dizzy today, so that's a good sign," she replies. She's never mentioned to me that she's felt that way lately, and it's a little upsetting that I didn't know. The nurse asks Grandma if she needs another blanket or anything to drink before she leaves to check on another patient.

"Grandma, why—" I start to say.

"I don't want to worry you with my petty side effects," she replies, answering my question before I can even finish asking it

"Any side effect you have is not petty. I am living with you to help you to make things easier for you. You need to tell me these things," I respond.

"Okay, okay. I will from now on," she says as she struggles to keep her eyes open.

I grab my bag to head out to the waiting room. I've brought my list of possible donors for the silent auction so that I can make a few phone calls to solicit donations for the charity ball.

Before I sit down, I see Felicity and Vivian across the room. She looks a lot more tired today than she did last week, and she's sitting in a wheelchair. She is wearing a scarf today.

"Hey, Felicity, what's new?" I ask her. She seems to perk up a bit when I sit down next to her.

"Not much." I don't really know what else to say to her. Luckily, she breaks the silence. "Have you ever had one of those days when little things like walking into the next room take up all your energy and you feel so weak?" I nod my head. "Today is one of those days." Vivian pretends to be reading a magazine, but I know she is listening to our conversation.

I had many of those days during my own battle, and I remember them too well. It was really frustrating. "Don't give up, it will get better eventually," I say, putting my hand on her knee.

"Felicity Caldwell," the nurse beckons.

"Hang in there," I say as her mom wheels her into the next room.

I open my notes. The first person I call donates a timeshare. The second company donates a suite at the Natives game for up to thirty people. Two hours fly by, and I have thirteen donations on the books. I need to take a break from sitting down, so I grab my things and walk down the stark hallway to check on my grandma. She is awake.

"Another hour or so, and I'll be released," she says excitedly.

I smile back at her. "Then we get to go home to a delicious dinner that Jace prepared for us." I felt so bad about canceling our date tonight to help Grandma. He insisted on cooking a meal instead at my grandma's house, so that I could be close by if she needed anything. He's so thoughtful.

*****

I walk arm in arm with Grandma up the front steps to the door. She already seems weaker, and it's just her second treatment. As we walk inside, I can smell lemon and herbs in the air. "You know, I'm really not that hungry. If you could just get me a small plate of food, I'd like to sit in the living room and watch some TV," Grandma says. I know she is trying to give me privacy with Jace. I help her get situated in a chair, then walk down the hall into the kitchen. Jace is pulling a dish out of the oven. A gorgeous arrangement of blue forget-me-nots sits in a clear vase with a white ribbon tied around it. The flowers instantly remind me of my mom, as they were her favorite. "Are these from you?" I ask excitedly, as I lean over to smell them. He sets the dish down, takes the oven mitts off, and walks over to me. I pull a little card from the envelope sticking out of the flower arrangement.

"I wish I could take credit for them. These came about an hour ago," he replies before he kisses my forehead.

As I read the card, my smile fades and I rip it up. If they weren't my mom's favorite flowers, I would chuck them in the garbage. "I take it they aren't for your grandma?" he asks.

"No." I know Quin is trying to make up for the other night. He hasn't bought me flowers since I had chemotherapy. The last thing I want to do is think about him, and now I have this constant reminder of him in the kitchen. "I think my grandma would enjoy them more," I say as I pick up the bouquet to carry it into the living room. I hope this doesn't ruin our evening, or make Jace second-guess dating me.

When I return to the kitchen, he has two plates ready for us. "Why don't you take these to the patio, and I will take this one to your grandma?" he offers.

"Okay," I say, as I take the plates from him. Roasted red potatoes, lemon chicken, and some colorful, sautéed vegetables are arranged on each plate. I push the back door open with my hip. Jace has set up candles all over the deck, and a beige paisley-patterned tablecloth that I have never seen before covers the patio table.

The sun is setting in the horizon, and there is a warm breeze. It's perfect and romantic. I can't help but smile, and I feel important that he would take the time and effort to set up something so nice for me. I am so caught up in admiring everything that I don't even hear Jace walk out. He sets down a pitcher of deep red liquid. I wrap my arms around his neck and kiss him. "Thank you," I say sincerely. He smiles, and we sit down to eat.

"How was your day?" I ask him.

"Better, now that I'm with you," he replies.

I grin. "This chicken is delicious," I say, as he fills my glass from the pitcher. I take a sip. It tastes fruity and sweet.

"I found a recipe for a nonalcoholic sangria, only because I noticed that every time we've been around alcohol you don't drink," he says. I am amazed at how he pays attention to details. I don't think I have ever dated a guy that was so observant. It's nice.

"Anything eventful happen at the shelter today?" I ask.

Jace winces. "Do you think we can keep work-related discussions at the office? The shelter is a huge part of my life, but it's important for me to take a break when I can." His voice is gentle.

"Yeah, sure, I understand," I respond, but I suddenly feel like he's shutting me out. I'm so used to swapping work stories with Quin that it might take some adjusting to not do the same thing with Jace.

By the time we finish eating, the sky is shimmering with stars. I carry our empty plates back into the house and check on Grandma. She is fast asleep in her bedroom. "So, what do you want to do now?" I ask Jace as I come back outside. He pulls me close to him. Our lips are just inches apart, and I stare into his blue eyes. The tension is running high. We kiss. Passionately.

After a moment, Jace pulls back, smiling. "I have to get going," he whispers. I kiss him one more time. He hasn't told me about the conversation between him and my grandma yet, like he said he would. But the night has been so perfect that I don't want to press the issue.

Chapter 20

About two weeks have gone by since the new chemo started. Grandma's hair is completely gone now, but the colorful, patterned scarves look great on her. She hasn't been responding to this new chemo well, though. She has been throwing up, and she's very dizzy. She sleeps a lot. It's really hard to see her like this. I hate leaving her when I have to go to work. Jace has been really great, and he lets me take an hour-long lunch so I can go home and check on her, and Ariana has been coming over to help, too.

Jace and I have been spending a lot of time together outside of work, which has been helpful in taking my mind off Grandma, and I haven't heard from Quin at all. It's kind of weird not talking to him these days, because we were best friends for so long.

I wheel Grandma into the hospital. She has another treatment today. Jace has decided to come with us, which I'm thankful for. She sleeps during most of the infusion because the treatments are really wearing her out.

Jace and I hold hands in the waiting room. I noticed he has been looking around, taking everything in. It can be daunting to sit in a room full of cancer patients, especially if it's your first time. He's probably wondering what the stories are of each patient there.

Finally, the nurse calls us in to take Grandma's blood work. She goes over the usual list of questions with Grandma, to find out what symptoms she has been experiencing. Twelve, so far. She has lost ten pounds, too. When they finish her checkup, we go back to the waiting room. Not even ten minutes later, the nurse calls us back into the exam room. This is weird. Normally, we would head right back to the infusion area. Instead, the nurse says, "Faustina, your blood counts are too low, and you need a transfusion right away. We are going to get you set up in a room so that you can get comfortable, but we won't be able to do the transfusion for a couple of hours, and then you will need to stay overnight." That explains why she has been so tired and dizzy.

Jace places his arm around my shoulder. It's like he can sense that I am distressed. Grandma doesn't look worried at all, just exhausted. Her shoulders hunch as she sits in the wheelchair, making her look weaker, but she still keeps a positive attitude. "Okay, as long as I can still get room service, including the VIP package," she jokes.

The nurse takes us to a small room past the infusion center. Grandma is given a hospital gown to change into, and I text my sister to let her know what's going on. Both she and my dad are working right now.

"Abrielle, would you mind running home and picking up my toothbrush and a few other things for me?" Grandma asks when I'm off the phone.

"Sure," I reply, but I really don't want to leave her in case something bad happens.

"I'm going to be okay," she reassures me.

I try to smile at her. "I know," I say, even though I don't believe that anymore. Cancer patients get transfusions all the time: that's not what I'm concerned about. It's how much the chemo is draining her energy. She seems to be dying right before my eyes.

Grandma gets situated in the hospital bed and pretends to be interested in some TV show. When Jace drives me back to her house, I grab the belongings she's asked for, then I run upstairs to get a few things for myself. I'm not looking forward to another night in the hospital, but I'm not leaving my grandma alone this time, either.

I walk quickly down the stairs to see Jace waiting for me in the family room. "Breathe," he says gently as he takes my free hand in his. "I have to go in to work for a bit, but I will go back to the hospital tonight for a little while, okay?"

I nod my head, and he kisses me. I let the bag I packed drop to the floor and wrap both my arms around his neck. Our kiss changes from gentle to passionate. I guide him backward until he is pressed up against the wall as we kiss. "Remember how I said I was waiting until marriage?" I say as he kisses my neck.

"Mmhhhmm."

"Well, I've changed my mind." His lips meet mine again, and I reach for his belt buckle. It comes undone easily.

"Abrielle, wait." He stops my hands with his. His eyes search mine. "We shouldn't be doing this. Believe me, I want to. I *really* want to. But you promised your mom..." He pauses.

I bite my lower lip. He's right. I sigh. What the heck was I thinking? I can't believe I almost did that. I mean, I really like Jace, but I don't love him—at least not yet.

He grasps my hands tighter. "I think you're under a lot of stress right now, and I wouldn't want you to do something you will regret."

"Thank you," I respond quietly, then I turn to pick up my overnight bag. That must have been really hard for him to do, but I'm glad he respects me.

*****

A classic rock song plays quietly through my headphones to help me tune out the beeping machine that Grandma is hooked up to. She finished her transfusion two hours ago, and now she lies asleep in the hospital bed in front of me. The doctors want to monitor her overnight. Her hospital room is nothing special: the top half of the walls are white, while the bottom half is plastered with patterned wallpaper. The small couch I'm sitting on was comfortable for the first twenty minutes, but now it feels like a rock. I bite my nails and stare at Grandma, lost in a daydream of a time when she wasn't sick.

"Abrielle," Quin says, surprising me as he walks into the room, snapping me out of my daydream. He's the last person I expected to see walk through the hospital door. "I just came by to drop off a card for your grandma. Your sister told me what happened. I didn't know you would be here, too."

"It's okay."

"How are you holding up?" he asks as he sits down on the couch next to me. Suddenly it seems even smaller than it did before. He puts his arm up on the back of the couch and I lean into him. I haven't talked to him in about three weeks, but I'm glad he's here now. "I really miss you," he says softly and lets his arm fall from the back of the couch to my shoulders.

As much as I'm trying not to cry, my emotions get the best of me. I cry because I'm scared of losing my grandma. I cry because I almost gave it up today with Jace. I cry because a little part of me is still frustrated that Quin didn't even try to make it work with me. I cry because I'm overwhelmed with my life right now. He hands me a tissue from the little table next to him. He doesn't say anything, but he doesn't need to. He just holds me and that's enough.

*****

"Ahem."

I open my eyes. I must have fallen asleep on Quin's shoulder. Jace is standing in the doorway. He looks upset. I can only imagine what this must look like to him. I forgot he was coming back to the hospital tonight. Grandma stirs, but she doesn't wake up. Quin and I quickly stand up from the couch.

"You're still dating this guy?" Quin asks scornfully.

I clear my throat rather than answering the question. "Thanks for stopping by," I say, hoping Quin will get the hint and leave. But instead he kisses my cheek, which makes me blush. This is so uncomfortable.

"Call me if you need *anything*. I'm here for you, no matter what," Quin finally says. I nod my head and stare at the ground, not wanting to make eye contact with either one of them right now.

Quin pauses in front of Jace. "And you. I did a background check on you," Quin says coldly.

"Okay," Jace replies smoothly. I can tell he looks a little worried, but he is trying to maintain a confident demeanor.

Quin is trying to intimidate him. He shakes his head back and forth at Jace. "There's something off about you," he says, then he steps around Jace.

A look of concern flashes across Jace's face. "What is he talking about?" I demand when Quin has left the room.

"He's just making stuff up. He wants to break us up because he still likes you." Jace's explanation doesn't ring true.

"Well, I know Quin isn't a fan of us dating, but he wouldn't just make something up like that, either."

"What was going on between you two when I walked in? Do you just cuddle up with any guy you see?" he asks somewhat angrily, clearly trying to change the subject.

I guess I might have been cuddling with Quin, but the question still catches me off guard. "He was just comforting me."

"Right. Sorry to interrupt whatever was going on between you two." Jace drops a brown paper bag on the counter and then storms out of the hospital room.

What the heck just happened? Jace is clearly jealous and upset that I fell asleep on Quin's shoulder. I look over at Grandma. She has slept through all the commotion. I grab the brown paper bag off the counter and open it. Inside is a piece of homemade chocolate cake, a plastic fork, and an individual bottle of milk. I sigh. Jace is so sweet. As soon as I saw Quin tonight, I had thought he was the only person who could understood what I'm going through, but Jace keeps proving that he understands, too. I pick up my phone and send him a thank-you text for the late-night snack, but I decide to wait until tomorrow to actually call and talk to him.

Chapter 21

Dad shows up at the hospital early the next morning, so I go home to shower, and while I'm there, I decide to make a nice breakfast for Jace as a peace offering. I set the table for two, then text him to come over and talk, but he never replies. I am just about to make a plate for him to take over to his house, when there is a knock on the door. It's Jace. He looks good, even in a pair of jeans and a T-shirt.

"I'm sorry about last night. I have been really stressed out lately, and when I saw Quin there with you, I just freaked out," he says.

"I'm sorry, too. I should be more aware of how I interact with Quin. I don't want to send the wrong message to him."

His arms envelop me. We kiss, and everything seems right again.

"So, where is this breakfast you promised me?" he asks with a smile. I take his hand and lead him into the kitchen.

"You might need to warm it up." As Jace makes up his plate, his phone buzzes in his pocket several times, but he ignores it.

"What have you been stressed about?" I ask.

"Some...family stuff," he replies as he puts his plate in the microwave. I didn't know he was having family issues. But come to think of it, he never really talks about his family—and I have never been over to his house.

"Anything I can help with?" I offer.

"There's something I have been meaning to tell you," he begins. "I've been putting it off—"

"Hello?" Ariana calls from the front door.

I give Jace an *I'm sorry, I had no idea she would be here* look. "Hold that thought."

"It's not that big of a deal. I can talk to you about it later."

"Okay, whenever you're ready."

I wonder what he has been putting off telling me as Ariana walks into the kitchen. "Oh, you made breakfast for your favorite sister!" she exclaims as she hugs me.

"Yep. Just for you," I say as I pull out a chair for her. "Grandma didn't get released yet?"

"Oh, you know how they like to keep people at the hospital longer than they need to."

"Any idea of a release time?"

"They said she could come home this afternoon, which most likely means this evening," Ariana replies haughtily. She starts making up a plate of breakfast food.

I sit down next to her. "Are you okay?" I ask, placing my hand on her shoulder.

"This just sucks."

I nod my head in understanding. "Yep."

She exhales deeply. "Grandma is the third person that I have to watch go through this. The worst part is, I can see that she is in pain, but she is so stubborn that she won't even admit it. I want to know how to help her...and...I don't want to see her lose to cancer. It's not fair."

I wish I could reassure my sister by telling her that our grandma is not going to die, but I can't. I hug her instead.

Jace sits down across from us. "Beating cancer isn't about living or dying. It's about how well you live each day, your attitude, and what you make of it. Staying positive—that's winning. And that's what your grandma is doing."

My sister nods as she stares at her plate. I can tell she is trying not to cry. I'm also fighting back tears. I've never thought of winning the battle against cancer from that perspective before. He has a point. I reach for his hand across the table.

Ariana wipes her eyes. "Do you mind if I stay here on the weekends?" she asks.

"Not at all—it would be great to have you around more." She has been here a lot anyway during the week, so it makes sense that she would want to spend the night more often, too.

* * * * *

I gaze around the coffee shop. My eyes need a break from the computer screen. I have been sitting here for two hours soliciting donations for the charity ball. We are another week closer to the event and doing well with donations. Thank goodness it's almost the weekend. Ariana is at home with Grandma, who seems to be doing better lately.

The coffee shop has had pretty steady traffic for a Thursday afternoon. There's been almost at least one person in line. Two teenagers now share an oversized beanbag in one corner, and an older gentleman reads a newspaper at a table nearby. Three young moms share a bigger table to my left, their babies unusually quiet for how little they are. The women share stories and laugh, catching up on life.

The bell on the door chimes, and Reagan walks in. "Oh, hey, Abrielle," she says kindly as she sits down across from me. She recently traded her purple highlights for dark red ones. She is wearing a maroon tank top with lacy straps that match her hair. Gold earrings, longer than her hair, dangle from her ears.

"Hey, we should go shopping together sometime," I tell her. "You always wear the cutest clothes."

"I was just about to hit up a few stores. Do you want to come along?"

"Really? Okay, sure. I could use a break from this."

She gets in line to order her coffee while I put my notes and computer away.

I feel like there has been a tension between us in the office ever since the cookout at my grandma's house, so this might be a chance to get to know her better. Behind the coffee shop there are a couple strip malls with stores and a few restaurants. Reagan pays for her coffee and we walk across the parking lot toward the stores together.

"I've never been here before," I comment as we walk toward a store window filled with summer accessories.

"There are some really great deals here!" Reagan exclaims as she holds the door open for me. It smells like someone has sprayed a floral perfume around the store. A young sales associate decked out in fashion jewelry hands us each a little basket. "Let me know if you need help finding anything," she says with a warm smile.

"This is my favorite store," Reagan says. I'm overwhelmed as I look around. There are all kinds of jewelry, sunglasses, purses, scarves, and shoes sorted by color. There is a table of blue items to my right, purple items in front of me, and red to my left. We each head to different displays. Reagan goes to the red items first while I go to the orange. A flowered silk scarf catches my eye. Grandma has been wearing the same two scarves that I lent her for the past five weeks. I'm sure she is sick of them. I put the scarf in my basket and look around for more. I spot another one decorated with various shades of blue swirls. I add that and a solid gray one to my basket.

"These would look cute on you," Reagan says as she holds up a group of bracelets. Each one is beaded in slightly different textures and shades of pink. I try them on. "See?" They do go well with the pale pink top I'm wearing.

We pay for our items and head back outside. It has started drizzling a bit, but luckily all the stores are close together and there's an awning over the sidewalk.

The next store we go into is a clothing boutique with some very interesting items. I probably would not have come in if I weren't with Reagan. She holds up a men's green shirt with gold screen-printing on the front. "Jace would like this. You should get it for him," she says.

It doesn't look like anything I have ever seen him wear. I shrug my shoulders doubtfully.

"Okay, I'll get it for him then."

"Are you guys good friends?" I feel stupid asking that, since Jace and I have been dating awhile. I should know who his friends are. He has never mentioned Reagan in conversations, though.

"Yeah, we are. Plus his birthday is Saturday."

I really hate that I still forget things all the time. I thought the doctors were joking when they said memory loss was a side effect of chemo, but years later, I still have trouble remembering things. Jace mentioned his birthday a few weeks ago, but I've totally spaced about it. What the heck am I going to get him?

"I'm throwing a party for him at the sports bar on Kettle Street," Reagan says. "You can make it, right?" I think she can see the confusion on my face because she adds, "I just figured, since you are so busy with your grandma, I would do all the planning. I guess I should have mentioned it to you."

It's a nice gesture, but it's really bizarre. *I'm* his girlfriend. I should be the one planning a party for him. "Yeah, I can make it."

"Good, because it's a surprise, so I was hoping you could act like you're taking him out for a birthday dinner, and then all his friends will be there to surprise him when you get to the restaurant."

"Okay."

"Oh, and can you invite Quin? He's hot." Reagan grins.

"I'm not sure if that's a good idea. He and Jace don't really get along."

"Well, maybe I can call and invite him as my date. I'll make sure to keep him distracted from Jace," she says coyly.

"Um, yeah, okay," I say uneasily as I fumble in my phone for Quin's number. I send it to Reagan reluctantly as we continue looking around the store. She picks out a few things for me to try on, and a few shirts for herself.

"There's only one dressing room," the sales clerk tells us.

"It's okay, we can share," Reagan offers. I don't feel one hundred percent comfortable sharing a dressing room with her, but it shouldn't be that big of a deal; we are only trying on some shirts. She tries on a black and silver tank top first, and

I try on a gray one. We look at each other in the mirror. Her tank is really tight, and low cut. "Love it," she says. "You look hot, too."

"Thanks." I force a smile. But I do like the shirt she's picked for me. The material is summery.

"Try this one on now." She hands me a blue shirt that hangs off one shoulder, while she grabs a white one to try on. "So, have you and Jace had sex yet?" Her casual bluntness startles me.

"No," I reply as I try to adjust the shirt. I wear tank tops a lot, but I feel like I am dressed for a nightclub with this on. I have no intention of telling her that Jace and I have decided to wait.

"Oh. I thought you would have done it by now."

What is that comment supposed to mean? Does she know something about Jace that I don't? "Oh my gosh, what time is it? I told my grandma I would be home by two," I lie. I want to get out of here. This is totally uncomfortable.

Reagan checks her phone. "It's one thirty."

"I better get going, then."

I buy the gray tank top. Reagan buys everything she tried on—plus the shirt for Jace.

"Thanks for inviting me to shop with you today," I say as I search for my keys.

"No problem. It was fun. We should do this again sometime," she says.

Or not, I think to myself. I would like to stick to being just work friends with her. She opens her arms for a hug goodbye, then we go our separate ways to our cars.

Chapter 22

I stand in the cafeteria of the shelter looking around. Dinner ended about an hour ago, and a large group of people is hanging out, waiting for the dormitories to open. A few little kids are chasing each other around the perimeter of the room, while two older guys sit at a table, looking irritated by the noise and commotion. Isaac walks across the room toward me at the same time Reagan does. "You're here late today," I say to her.

"Yeah, I had a few things to finish up. Isaac, you're coming to Jace's birthday party this Saturday, right?" He nods his head. "Good. Alright, I need to get home. Have a good night!"

"'Bye," Isaac and I say in unison. Once she is out of earshot, I can't help but grill Isaac about her relationship with Jace. "Have you guys all been friends long?"

"Yeah, for a few years," he replies. I had picked up on Isaac and Jace, but not on Reagan being close with them.

"It's weird that she is planning his birthday party, right? I mean, as his girlfriend, I think that's kind of my job."

"Yeah, it's a little weird." Isaac doesn't seem that interested in talking about it. "Hey, do you mind if I study for my econ test tonight?" he asks nervously. We aren't supposed to bring in outside things to do during our shifts, as we are supposed to stay aware of what's going on around the building.

"You're taking a summer class?"

"Yeah, my final is tomorrow morning, and I need all the study time I can get."

"I don't mind."

He sighs in relief. "Thanks. I'm going to grab my books out of my car. Be right back."

"Sleeping dorms will open in five minutes," Giselle announces. Her shift will end once the cafeteria is cleared. I walk down to the dormitories and wait.

*****

Jace holds the door open for me, and we walk into the sports bar. It's crowded with young people and a few families eating dinner. Sports memorabilia from all types of teams decorates the walls. About thirty different-sized TVs are mounted throughout the place. Different games and sporting events are showing, with the more popular games on the bigger TVs. A hostess dressed in all black greets us. I glance around, looking for Reagan. I finally spot her over in the corner with a group of people.

"I think I see someone we know," I say to the hostess as I grab Jace's hand. I lead him past tables filled with people eating, drinking, laughing, and watching TV. As we get closer to Reagan's table, he realizes it's a party for him. He seems genuinely surprised. Colorful birthday balloons are tied to an empty chair. Isaac, Silas, and Holden are gathered around the table waiting to greet him.

"Happy birthday!" Reagan calls enthusiastically over the noise as she hugs Jace. "Hey, thanks for getting him here," she says as she hugs me, too. It's a relief to see that Quin's not here. I know Reagan invited him.

We all grab chairs around the table. "Hey, can you scoot down one so Abrielle can sit next to me?" Jace says to Reagan.

"Of course." She moves down to the next chair. "I already ordered the first round of shots!" she exclaims. They are in the middle of the table, and everyone except me grabs one. "To the birthday boy," Reagan toasts. They all down the alcohol.

"You're not drinking?" Holden asks me.

"No, I'm good." For some reason I don't want everyone to know that I'm not twenty-one yet.

"More for me," Reagan says as she grabs the extra shot.

"Twenty-four. Man, you're getting old," Silas says to Jace.

"Look who's talking. You have, like, fifteen years on me," Jace jokes back.

We all place our food orders, and Holden orders another round of shots for everyone. I didn't know it was going to be this kind of party. This should be interesting.

"I'll be right back," I excuse myself and head toward the restroom. A few moments later, Reagan walks in behind me. I didn't hear her following me. She pulls some red lipstick out of her purse as we stand in front of the mirror.

"I wish you would drink with us," she says as she applies the lipstick.

"Actually, I'm not twenty-one yet."

"What?!" she shrieks in shock, and then laughs. "Had me fooled." She puts the cap back on the lipstick and presses her lips together. "Well, with all this alcohol, you never know what secrets might come out of the bag tonight," she says mysteriously, then leaves. I wonder what that was all about.

I finish up in the bathroom and head back to the table. Silas and Isaac are engaged in conversation about some action movie that just came out. Reagan is taking pictures of everyone on her phone. Once I sit back down, Jace rests his hand on my leg and leans in toward me.

"Thank you for planning this for me," he whispers. His breath is warm against my ear.

"I wish I could take credit for it, but Reagan actually did everything."

"What? What do you mean?" he asks in surprise.

"I didn't even know about this until a few days ago, when she invited me," I whisper back. Jace looks confused. Reagan is hanging all over Isaac, so she probably can't hear us over the music and noise.

"If it makes you feel any better, I was looking forward to a quiet, romantic dinner with just you tonight."

I smile. "It does," I say before we lock lips.

"Hey, guys, get a room," Holden jokes. I notice Reagan staring at us, but before she can say anything, the server brings out our food.

"We need one more round of shots, please," she tells him.

"I'm out," Isaac says.

"Yeah, I'm done after this drink, too," Silas adds as he holds up his whiskey and Coke.

"Fine, three shots then, please," Reagan says as she grabs a French fry from Isaac's plate. I can't help but notice that she is being a huge flirt. She's not like this at work. She's usually quiet and sticks to her job.

"These ribs are really good. Do you want to try one?" Jace looks at me.

"No thanks," I reply. It's nice of him to offer.

"I'll take one," Reagan says, and he reluctantly breaks off a piece for her.

When the server drops off the third round of shots, the three of them clink glasses and drink. I didn't know Jace was so into alcohol. He's had one or two drinks at past events, but the way they are going tonight, he will be drunk in no time. But as long as he doesn't act too differently when he's drunk, it won't bother me.

"Hey, can anyone pick up my shifts next week? I'm going be out of town," Holden asks. Jace shoots him a look.

"Oh, sorry, I forgot. Jace doesn't like to talk about work outside of work, hold on." Holden takes out his phone and sends a group text to Isaac, Silas, and me. I can't help but laugh. Jace rolls his eyes and shakes his head.

"Alright, kids, I have to get home," Silas says as he stands up. He never ordered food, just a drink.

"What, is it past your bedtime, old man?" Isaac says. Silas snickers. Reagan runs around the table to give him a hug good-bye. He shakes hands with Jace, and waves to the rest of us. I think tonight is the first time I've seen Silas relaxed. He's always so serious at work.

"We should play a drinking game!" Reagan shouts excitedly when Silas is gone.

"I'm twenty-four, not twenty-one, so let's take it easy," Jace replies.

"Oh, you're no fun at all," Reagan says mockingly in a British accent. She grabs Isaac's hand. "Come to the bar and get another shot with me," she pleads. I didn't know they were together. Maybe they aren't. She has been flirting with him most of the night, though. Whatever is going on between them, they sure do keep it professional at work.

"Someone has to drive," Isaac says reluctantly.

"Ugh, fine. Guys?" she says as she looks toward Jace and Holden. Jace shakes his head, but Holden stands up.

"When a pretty girl asks you to do a shot with her, you do it," he says to Isaac and Jace as he and Reagan head over to the bar.

"How did you do on your test?" I ask Isaac.

"I got a ninety-three percent."

"That's awesome!"

When Holden and Reagan come back to the table, she asks, "So, Abrielle, do you want to get married someday?" Jace chokes on his drink.

"Yeah, I'd like to eventually."

Isaac wraps his arm around Reagan's waist and pulls her closer to him, but she keeps talking. "Do you think you could ever marry a guy who is divorced?"

Jace is still coughing, but she ignores him.

"Are you okay?" I ask him as I put my hand on his shoulder.

"Yes," he finally chokes out.

Isaac whispers something in Reagan's ear, and she nods her head and smiles.

"Anyone want to play bean bags?" Holden changes the subject.

"Yes!" Reagan shrieks as she throws her hands up in the air. She seems pretty drunk. She grabs Isaac's hand and pulls him out towards the patio while Holden follows, Jace looks at me.

"I'm not that good at bean bags," I tell him.

"It's okay, we can just hang out here," he says as he puts his arm around me.

"Are you and Reagan really good friends?" I ask. I want to know what kind of friend he considers her to be.

"I know her pretty well. Actually, she and I—"

"Last round!" Holden is back at the table, and places a shot glass in front of Jace. "All the boards outside are taken," Holden adds.

"I'm seriously done after this," Jace replies.

Reagan and Isaac reach the table and take a sip of their drinks. "Hey, let's go to a different bar," Reagan suggests, looking at me. It's obvious she knows I won't be able to get in.

"Yeah, maybe. Let's go out front and figure it out." Holden looks over at Reagan.

We all pay our bills, and Jace grabs my hand as we walk outside. Holden lights up a cigarette.

"Well, where to?" Reagan asks. She's slurring her words a little. I look over at Jace.

"You can go if you want, it's your birthday. I don't mind."

"I'm not going to ditch you," he says as he leans in to kiss me. His kiss is wet and sloppy. He is clearly drunk. He keeps trying to kiss me longer, which makes me feel awkward, since all his friends are watching us. I gently stop him and grab his hand.

"Maybe we should all just head home instead," Isaac offers, clearly realizing no one should be drinking anymore.

"Fine. Who can drive me home tonight?" Reagan asks loudly. She looks around at all the guys. "Jace, can you give me a ride?"

"I'll give you one," Isaac offers before Jace can respond.

She looks from Jace to Isaac before she finally says, "Okay." Did she really just imply that she wanted Jace to take her home—right in front of me?

"Thanks for coming out, guys," Jace says.

"No problem, bro." Holden flicks his cigarette butt to the ground.

We all exchange good-byes, then Jace and I get into my car, and we head home. He looks a little tired as I drive. "So, what was all that about with Reagan?" I ask.

"I don't know. She was drunk," he replies. "I'm sorry the night turned out the way it did. I'm sure you didn't want to hang out with those guys all night."

"What are you talking about? It's your birthday. As long as you had fun, that's all that matters."

He half-smiles. "You're an amazing girlfriend."

I love it when he calls me that. "Maybe we can grab brunch tomorrow? How does ten a.m. sound?" I ask as we pull up in front of his house.

"Anything you want." He leans over to kiss me. His breath tastes like cinnamon and alcohol. "Good night." He kisses my forehead once more, then gets out of the car. I pull forward two houses and park in front Grandma's driveway. That was a strange evening.

Chapter 23

I walk up the newly painted porch steps and knock on the front door. Jace and I were supposed to go to brunch at ten, and it's now ten thirty. I am anxious to give him his birthday present. I never had the chance to give it to him yesterday. I've wrapped the skydiving tickets in a little box, then tied it with a blue bow. Blue is his favorite color, and he had mentioned a few weeks ago that he always wanted to go skydiving.

After a few moments, Jace answers the door, wearing only lounge shorts. He seems surprised to see me. "Hey, is everything okay?" he asks.

"You forgot about brunch." I lean in for a kiss.

"I'm so sorry," he says. He looks like he just woke up.

"How are you feeling this morning?"

"I'm okay. Can you give me twenty minutes to get ready, and I'll come pick you up?"

I had expected him to invite me in to wait for him. But before I can reply, I hear a female voice ask, "Who's here?" Reagan suddenly appears in the doorway, wearing short compression shorts and a low-cut tank top. Her mouth forms a smile when she sees me.

I look from Reagan to Jace and back.

"It's not what it looks like," Jace offers.

"Right, the two of you are just hanging out—half-naked," I say angrily. It suddenly makes sense. She was flirting with him last night, and now she's here. I can't believe he would do this to me. I storm down the front steps, feeling sick to my stomach. Then I notice the purple challenger parked in front of the house. It must be Reagan's car! How many times has this happened before?!

"Abrielle, wait! I can explain."

I stop and turn around. "There is nothing to explain, Jace. It's obvious what's going on."

"It's really not what you think. Please. Come inside and I will tell you everything."

How much is there to tell? I don't want to hear the details. Part of me wonders what lies or excuses he has to say about this, but another part of me doesn't want to hear it. I walk across his front lawn. He runs to catch up to me and blocks my path.

"Abrielle, I would never do anything to hurt you," he says as he looks into my eyes. I feel so sick; I might puke all over him. "Nothing happened between me and Reagan."

I don't believe him. "What's to explain, then, if nothing happened?" Hurt and anger fill my wavering voice.

"C'mon back to the house, and I'll tell you everything."

Reagan is watching from the front doorway. "You really should listen to the whole story," she calls.

I reluctantly walk toward the house. As angry as I am, we would probably talk about this eventually, so I'd rather get it over with now. I give her an evil stare. I can't believe I tried to be friends with her. We get inside and Reagan and I sit on separate couches. I have never been inside Jace's house before, but I'm too angry to look around and take everything in.

"Please, just let me tell you the whole story," he pleads.

"I'm sitting here, aren't I?" I say harshly as I lean back into the couch.

He ignores my tone, and begins, "Remember how I told you that I recently became a U.S. citizen?"

"Yeah." I don't get what this has to do with Reagan. I look over at her. She is looking down at her hands.

Jace continues, "Well, I didn't tell you exactly *how* I became a citizen. I am legal now, because three months ago, when I started getting those letters from the government, I asked Reagan to marry me at the courthouse. It was the only way I knew I would be able to stay here."

My eyes widen. I gasp and stand up. "So let me get this straight. You have been married the *whole* time that we have been dating?" I shriek.

"It's really more of a business deal," Reagan chimes in. Her hands are folded in her lap. "We started getting questioned by the government right away, so we agreed to live together so that it looks more legit," she adds.

The more she talks, the more nauseated and outraged I feel. I want to just get up leave, but my feet feel glued to the floor. I am in shock.

Jace walks over to me. "It's honestly just a business deal."

"A *business deal?* So you get to stay in America, and she gets what, payments from you or something?" Neither of them says anything. "Are you kidding me?" I yell. I am outraged and disgusted. "Marriage is not a business deal—it's a commitment. A serious commitment!" I start to walk toward the front door.

"It's just a piece of paper. It means nothing to me."

I whip around. "A piece of paper? Tell every couple whose marriage is built on love, that their relationship is just a piece of paper. You don't get to redefine marriage so that it's convenient for you. You're ridiculous. Both of you!" The words spew out of my mouth loudly and passionately. Jace doesn't try to stop me from leaving this time.

Hot tears roll down my face as I cut across the neighbors' lawns back to Grandma's house. I run upstairs to my bedroom. Luckily, my family is in the backyard. Maybe this is all a dream. Maybe I will just wake up and everything will be fine. I lie down on my bed and start to cry. Jace had so many opportunities to tell me the truth and he didn't. We had even talked about being honest with each other, too. I can't wrap my mind around how he thought this would be okay. It takes me a few minutes to catch my breath. My hurt turns to anger. I need to vent.

I grab my phone and call Jocelyn. "Hey, can you come over today?" I ask.

"Paolo surprised me this weekend, and we drove down to Myrtle Beach!" That's her favorite beach, and it's a few hours away.

I want to be happy for her, but I can't find it in me right now. "Okay, well, I will let you go, then."

She picks up on the sadness in my voice. "Bri, what's wrong?"

I sigh. "Jace and I are over. He—"

"Jocelyn, c'mon!" I hear Paolo calling her in the distance.

"Oh, shoot, I have to go. Can I call you later?" she asks. "I *promise* I will call you later."

"Mmm-hmm. 'Bye."

I scroll through my contacts list. I could call Natalia, but she might side with Jace, since she moved here from Italy. I stare at Quin's number for a minute. I can't call him to vent about Jace. It's still too awkward between us.

Just then a text message pops up from Jace. "Can we please talk?"

"I have nothing to say to you. Leave me alone," I reply. How am I supposed to work with him after all this? I don't even want to see him. I shake my head in frustration. I will have to figure out a way to overcome my emotions and be professional at the shelter. I need to stay here with Grandma, and I need a job.

"Abrielle," Grandma calls from the bottom of the stairs. Her voice sounds stronger today. I wipe the tears from my eyes. My head is pounding. "Just a minute!" I call out. I walk past my dresser and notice the picture of Quin's tattoo. What a joke the words suddenly seem. I don't feel strong at all right now. I feel betrayed, sick, weak, and hopeless. I can't believe that Jace lied to me. And on top of that, he thought that it would be okay to date someone while he was still married. But if he thinks marriage is just a piece of paper, then we had no future together anyways. Not that I'm ready to get married anytime soon, but why waste my time dating someone who doesn't share my beliefs?

I reach the bottom of the stairs "I feel really good today. Not *normal*, but the best I have felt in a while," Grandma says enthusiastically.

"That's great, Gram," I say as I hug her. I really am happy that she's feeling better, but I feel like crap.

"What's wrong?" she asks. I don't want to burden her with my drama when she's in such a good mood, so I look down and stay quiet.

"Abrielle," she insists.

"Jace and I got in a huge fight, and it's over."

"Oh honey, I'm so sorry." She hugs me again.

"Random hug fest? Why wasn't I invited?" Ariana asks as she approaches us. I roll my eyes. Nothing is ever serious with her. "Why is your face all red?" she asks.

"I don't know, maybe it's a sunburn." I don't want to say anything about Jace with Dad here. I try to change the subject. "So, Gram, since you have some energy today, is there anything you want to do?" I could use a distraction. Actually, I could use someone to vent to about Jace, more than I need a distraction.

"Why don't you go hang out with your friends today? You have been helping me so much, just go take a break." It's as if Grandma can read my mind.

"I'll probably go out with them later. I want to hang out here with you. Everyone's together."

She nods her head in agreement.

Chapter 24

Grandma wanted to use her energy to organize the rest of the house, so that's what we have been doing for the past few hours. We get through a lot. There are six boxes full of items to be donated in the garage, and her trash cans are full. It's fun going through all of her old things and listening to her talk about the memories attached to her belongings. I feel like I've gotten to know my grandpa a little better today.

The doorbell rings, and my stomach drops. I hope it's not Jace. I jump up to answer the door, because if it is him, I don't want my sister or dad to let him in. I hold my breath as I open the door. To my surprise it's Quin. "Hey, what are you doing here?" I ask.

"Jocelyn told me you really needed a friend right now. Wanna go for a ride?" He's wearing his favorite Natives cap. I nod my head. I'm so relieved he's here. He's the only other person I feel comfortable talking to about the whole situation, even if it might be a little awkward.

"Hey, guys, I'll be back later," I announce to my family as I grab my purse from the coffee table.

"Quin, do you want to join us for dinner later?" Dad asks.

"Only if you're not cooking, Mr. P," he jokes. I laugh. Dad is the worst cook ever. He tries, but the only thing he can do well is garlic mashed potatoes, although it's hard to mess that up.

"How about pizza?" Dad suggests.

"Sounds good. See ya later."

We walk out to his car. "Your grandma looked good today," Quin says.

"Yeah, she's having a really good day."

It's the days when you feel great in the midst of treatment that refuel your hope. He parked his truck across the street.

"So, Jocelyn wouldn't tell me what happened, just that I really needed to come over."

I smile weakly. Even when Jocelyn can't physically be there for me, she's still there for me. Quin walks around the passenger side to open the door for me. "This has nothing to do with my grandma. It all started this morning. I went over to Jace's house, and Reagan answered the door—"

Jace, who is yelling my name, cuts me off. He is jogging over toward us from his house. "Abrielle, wait! Can I talk to you for a few minutes before you go? Please." He is begging.

"Jace, you really hurt me, and I'm not ready to talk to you about it yet," I reply. The calmness in my voice surprises me.

"But you'll talk to Quin about it? We get in one little fight, and you run off to him. I knew there was something going on between you two."

I lose it. "Jace, you have no right to accuse *me* of cheating on *you*. You're married, and that's a big deal!" I am so angry I can't see straight.

"What? Dude, you're married?" Quin exclaims. His fists clench at his sides.

"You're not perfect, either, Quin. At least I didn't pressure her to have sex with me," Jace snaps back.

Before I can even try to stop him, Quin throws a punch at Jace's face, which sends him staggering backward. Jace wipes blood from his lip and lunges at Quin. Quin dodges out of the way, and Jace slams into the truck—he had too much momentum going to stop.

"C'mon, man. Bri can fight better than you do," Quin says haughtily, which just fuels the fire.

"Guys, stop," I chime in. They ignore me.

Jace swings at Quin, but Quin ducks, then hits him in the stomach. Twice. Jace groans. Then Quin jabs him in the face again. Jace does look pretty pathetic in a fight. He's strong enough for it to be an even match, but he just doesn't know how to fight.

"That's enough!" I yell, moving closer to them, but neither is listening. Jace swings again, and this time he manages to clip Quin in the jaw.

"Quin! Please stop," I beg.

He looks at me, then back at Jace, and backs away, rubbing his jaw. Jace looks like he intends to keep going, so I step in front of him. "Enough," I say firmly. Part of me wants to deck him, too, but he looks so feeble right now. "We are over. Please, just go home," I add.

"I'm so sorry. I didn't mean to…" he pleads. I stand in front of him with my arms crossed and shake my head in disbelief. He turns around and slowly walks back toward his house, clutching his stomach.

I turn around to deal with Quin. "I couldn't help it," he exclaims when he sees the look on my face. "The guy is a tool, and he hurt you. He had that coming."

I throw my hands up in the air in defeat. "Can't I just have a normal day?" I complain.

"There's no such thing as a normal day. Some days go the way you want, and some don't," Quin offers.

"Let's just get outta here."

He opens the door of his truck for me, and I climb in. I want to get as far away from here as possible.

"Hey, do you want to go to the shooting range and pretend that every target is Jace's face?" he asks in contempt.

I give him a weak smile. "Tempting, but nah. Let's go to the beach." I stare out the window, lost in thought. Quin knows me well enough not to bother me with questions right now. I'll talk when I'm ready. Twenty minutes go by without a word spoken between us.

"You'll never believe what I found the other day," Quin finally breaks the silence.

I'm not in the mood to guess. "What?"

"The CD you made me in high school," he replies as he turns the knob to disc one on his CD player.

I laugh as the first song starts to play. "No way!" I exclaim in excitement as high school memories flood my mind.

He cranks up the volume and the music we both liked in high school blares through the speakers. Quin starts singing along. He has a great voice, and he remembers every word. I can't help but crack up at the way he is moving along goofily to the beat. He's always known how to make me laugh. He lowers the volume a bit. "Hey, why did you make me this CD anyway?"

I think for a minute, then smile at the memory. "I gave it to you a few weeks before Homecoming. I was trying to give you the hint that I wanted you to ask me to the dance."

He smiles. I can tell he is trying to think back to that weekend. "I guess our timing was always off."

I nod my head.

We finally pull up to the beach. It's crowded, but then again it is Sunday. "C'mon, there's not as many people over this way," Quin says, leading me to the right. We leave our sandals in the car. There's only a little bit of pavement before the sand begins. I can smell the saltiness of the ocean and hear the crashing waves. The beach has always been a calming place for me.

Our feet hit the hot sand, and it fills in the cracks between my toes. We walk toward the water, passing by a few families with small children who are happily building sand castles. I wish I had brought my bathing suit with me. It's a balmy summer day, and there is a slight breeze. We start walking along the shoreline away from the crowds. The waves come up, soaking our ankles, and then recede. I love that feeling. Our feet leave a short path of footprints in the wet sand, until the waves wash them away moments later.

"So, what happened?" Quin asks. I tell him everything as we walk. Letting it all out makes me feel so much better. He listens attentively.

As I tell him the details toward the end of the story, tears roll down my cheeks. "Hey, it's okay," he says as he pulls me into a hug. I cry into his shoulder for a minute.

"I know you think I'm strong, but I'm not."

"Just because you're crying doesn't mean you're weak." He pulls back and lifts my chin so that I'm looking into his eyes. "It's when you're able to overcome difficulties at your weakest that makes you strong."

I nod my head in agreement, and wipe a tear away.

"Did you love him?" he asks.

I shrug. "I don't know... No... We just spent a lot of time together, and he was really there for me. I think that's why it hurts so much," I say.

"Do you think *he's* sitting at home crying right now?" he asks.

"Probably not... Well, maybe he's crying about what you did to him."

He smiles. "Yeah, you're welcome for that. He's not crying over you, so why should you cry over him? He's a scumbag who's not worth your tears. So, no more crying, okay?" He wipes the last tear from my cheek.

"Fine. I know how you get all uncomfortable when people cry in front of you."

"It's only when you cry. It breaks my heart to see you hurting," he says genuinely. He puts his arm around my shoulder, and we start to head back toward the car. This time he is closer to the ocean as we walk. We have gone so far that I can barely even see the crowds of people anymore.

"That was so cheesy."

"What? It's true." He smiles, as he looks me in the eye.

"Did you leave your phone in the truck?" I ask.

"Yeah, why?"

I grin and push him as hard as I can into the water.

He doesn't fall, but he stumbles, trying to catch his balance. I pushed him just as a wave was coming in, so the water has soaked most of his shorts. "You're gonna get it now!" he exclaims and runs toward me.

I scream and try to run away, but I don't get far. He grabs me at my waist from behind and lifts me off the ground. "You're getting dunked for that!"

"No, no, no!" I squeal. I push down on his hands to try and escape, but his grip is too tight. He throws me into the water. When I come up for air, I swing my arm along the surface and send a big splash his way. He splashes back, but I'm already soaked, so it doesn't matter. The water feels refreshing after walking in the sun for so long.

He sticks his hand out toward me. "Truce," he offers. Instead of shaking my hand, though, he grabs it and yanks me forward, pulling me toward him, deeper into the water. We are really close. Face-to-face. Neither of us moves. "That's a good look," he says as he moves closer.

"What?" I ask quietly.

"The seaweed in your hair," he replies as he reaches up and plucks it out.

Our eyes are locked. I clear my throat and move back, creating more space in between us. "I'm so thirsty, let's go," I finally say, ruining the moment. I start to move back toward the shore. I can hear him following me. If I would have waited a second longer, I think we would have kissed. I'm not ready for that.

Back on the shore, he takes his wet T-shirt off as we walk. "It's your lucky day, because I was about to go to the gym when Jocelyn called, so I have a clean shirt and towel in my gym bag that you can use."

"Thanks." It's not exactly comfortable walking back in soaking wet clothing. I wring out my hair as we walk.

When we get to his car, he hands me his towel and shirt. I quickly change in the parking lot, since he grabbed his clean gym shorts and ran to the restrooms. I fold the towel onto the car seat so I won't get his interior wet when I sit down. On the ride home, Quin pulls into the parking lot of a convenience store. "Stay here, I'll be back in a minute."

"Okay." I wonder what he is up to.

While he is in the store, I check my phone. There's a voice mail and a text from Jace. I delete the voice mail without listening to it. My finger hovers over the text message. Should I open it? Should I delete it without reading it? I click on it.

"I'm sorry about the things I said to Quin, and everything that happened today. Please let me know when you are ready to talk. I really hope we can work this out," it reads.

Unbelievable. There is nothing to work out. I delete the message, just as Quin comes back to the car. He tosses a bottle of strawberry lemonade onto my lap.

"What else did you get?" I ask as I twist the cap open.

"You'll find out later," he replies with a sneaky look on his face. Quin really likes to surprise people with things like gifts or by taking you somewhere and not telling you where you're going. I can only imagine what he's bought this time. We drive back to my grandma's house, listening to the CD I made him on the way.

We pull up to Grandma's at the same time as Dad. Grandma is in his passenger seat. She must have wanted to get out of the house. We both walk up to Dad's car to help with Grandma. Quin reaches out to her, and she links arms with him. She looks exhausted. Her green headscarf is falling off, but she doesn't seem to care. Dad grabs a pizza from the backseat.

"I knew she pushed herself too hard today," Ariana says as Quin walks Grandma back to her bedroom.

I help set out plates and drinks, then go to check on Grandma. "Hey, do you want me to bring a plate of food in here for you?" She has already changed into her pajamas. It's not even that late.

"No, I'm not hungry anymore, just tired. I felt great all day, and then all of a sudden..."

"I know," I say empathetically.

She sighs.

I sit on the edge of her bed next to her. She takes my hand in hers. "About Jace... I hope you can find it in your heart to forgive him."

I can't believe she just said that. "How can I forgive him after the way he lied to me and betrayed me?" I ask in shock.

"Abrielle, holding a grudge can be more toxic and painful to the person who needs to do the forgiving than to the one who did something wrong. I don't want you to carry that with you. I know it's not easy, but try to let it go."

I think she might be right, but I don't see how I can just let something like that go.

"You don't have to be friends with Jace anymore, or even like him, but promise me you will at least think about forgiving him?"

I nod my head. I will think about it, but I already know it won't be easy.

I stand up and tuck her in. "Good night Grandma." She mumbles something in reply as she closes her eyes.

Chapter 25

I lean back against the wall as I sit on my bed upstairs. It's late. Quin has left, Dad is sleeping, and I think Ariana is, too. I open the window next to my bed, even though the air-conditioning is on. The warm summer breeze comes swirling in. I pop a candy Hug into my mouth and sigh. I don't know how I am supposed to work with Jace or Reagan now after this morning. The office is too small to just avoid him all the time.

Someone knocks softly on the bedroom door, and it opens before I can respond. It's Ariana. I pull my knees up to my chest so she can sit on my bed.

"Quin told me about Jace."

I open up another piece of candy and pop it into my mouth.

"What are you going to do?"

"He was the best guy I ever dated—until I found out he was a liar. And he's married! He said it's just a piece of paper to him."

"I wonder if he and Reagan ever actually hooked up."

I glare at her. Of all the things she could say right now, that's what comes out of her mouth? "It doesn't matter whether they did or not, he should have told me he was married."

Ariana calmly opens a piece of candy.

"I should probably talk to him soon, so it doesn't get awkward at work. I don't know what to say, though. Grandma wants me to try to forgive him."

Ariana waves her hand in dismissal. "She's all hopped up on meds," she says through a mouthful of candy. "Did you buy this today?" She points to the half-eaten bag of candy spilled out on my bed.

"They're from Quin. Since he can't be here to give me a hug when I need one."

She laughs. "Is that what he told you when he gave them to you?"

I nod my head and laugh.

"He is so corny."

"I know," I say with a huge smile. That's one of the things I love about him, though.

*****

I am trying to concentrate at work, but I can't help but wonder if Jace will be here today. I just want to talk to him and get it over with. Luckily, I have been able to make rounds in order to avoid Reagan. She hasn't said anything to me. Half the day has gone by, and he still isn't here.

"Abrielle, can I see you in my office?" Dalilah asks.

I hesitantly walk into her office.

"Close the door please."

I do, and then sit down in the black plastic chair in front of her desk. "How are you?" she asks.

"I'm okay. How are you?" I'm not sure why she has called me in here.

Her smile fades. "I feel bad about everything that happened between you and my son. I'm so mad at him. I warned him that marrying Reagan would screw everything up for him if he ever found his dream girl." She seems genuinely upset. I'm caught off guard that she knows what happened. I'm not really sure how to respond. "Do you think you can ever forgive him?" she pleads.

"I'm going to try—"

"Oh good!" she gushes, cutting me off.

"But that doesn't mean we are getting back together."

She stares at me for a moment, as if vocalizing her reply in the correct way will somehow change my mind. "Jace really cares about you, Abrielle. I have never seen him this happy before."

I look down at my lap. It's a little weird to be having this conversation with his mom. "I was wondering if you can cut my schedule back to two shifts a week. Evening shifts. My grandma is getting sicker, and with all the side effects she's experiencing, I really need to be there for her."

"Yes, we can do that. I was just about to write up the next schedule." I'm sure Dalilah realizes that I'm trying to avoid Jace by working evening shifts. If I'm lucky, we will only be at the shelter for an hour at the same time each day. "Let me know if there is any other way we can help," she adds.

"I will," I say as I get up to leave. "Oh, and I need to drop out of the charity ball committee, too. I'll give Isaac my notes. I don't mind picking up the donations, but I just can't make it to the meetings." I need to minimize my time around Jace and Reagan if I want to get over him.

She looks disappointed, but nods her head. "I understand."

Chapter 26

As Grandma and I are about to leave the infusion room, I notice Felicity and Vivian in the corner. A balloon is tied to Felicity's chair. I wheel my grandma toward her. "Hey, Abrielle, this is my last round of chemo!" she exclaims proudly.

"That's so great!" I enthusiastically lean over to give her a hug. "Doesn't it feel amazing to be done?"

She nods and smiles.

"Congratulations," Grandma chimes in weakly.

"Thank you. Hopefully you will be celebrating your last chemo soon, too," Felicity says to Grandma.

She nods her head. "Take care," we both say as we depart. I remember my last day of chemo vividly. I was so excited. I actually made up a song about it being my last treatment as I left the hospital. I can't wait until it's Grandma's turn to say that. Thinking about that day fills me with hope.

When we get home, I set Grandma up in the living room with a glass of juice, a blanket, and the TV remote. She has been getting the chills the past couple days. I dealt with that, too. It's more than just the feeling that you need to cover up with a blanket. The chills from chemo pierce you to your bone, and no amount of blankets can fix it. They usually go away on their own after a few minutes, though. I sit down on the couch next to Grandma.

"Today is one of those days. I need someone to be strong for me," she says.

I wrap my arms around her and try not to cry.

"I try to tell myself that I can do this, but I feel like I'm never going to get better."

"You *can* do this. One day at a time," I say strongly, yet gently.

After a few minutes she falls asleep.

I need to figure out a way for her to better deal with the side effects. I grab my car keys and head out of the house to the library. I could just use my computer for the research I want to do, but I have always preferred books. I feel determined.

* * * * *

I walk through the front door with a stack of books, which instantly falls out of my hands when I see Grandma lying on the floor in the hallway. A wave of panic rushes over me, and I feel like my heart has stopped. She is lying next to a small pool of blood and vomit. I check her airways. She's still breathing, but she is definitely unconscious. I quickly dial nine-one-one. I was only gone for forty-five minutes—how could this could have happened?

It seems like it takes forever for the ambulance to arrive, but in reality it is only seven minutes. The paramedics rush in and check Grandma's vitals. They quickly transport her onto a gurney and move her out of the house. I swiftly grab my purse and lock the door.

Jace is standing outside on the sidewalk. There is a small scab on his lip where Quin hit him. He's the last person I want to see right now. "Abrielle, what happened?" He looks worried.

"I found her lying unconscious in the hallway," I say as I rifle through my purse for my car keys.

"Let me drive you to the hospital," he offers.

"No. I just need to find my keys."

He steps closer to me. "Your hands are shaking. I'm taking you."

The ambulance speeds off, sirens wailing. It probably would be safer if I accepted a ride from Jace to the hospital. "Fine, let's go," I say. We run down the street to his Jeep.

I stare out the window as we drive. Jace and I haven't talked in three days. His hand slips into mine, which is still shaking. His touch used to be comforting, but it's not so much anymore. I withdraw my hand and try not to cry. I am so worried about my grandma. I have no idea what happened. Maybe she just had a dizzy spell and fainted. Hopefully it's not something worse. I pull out my phone and text my sister to let her know what has happened.

"Listen, Abrielle. I should have been honest with you from the beginning. I never wanted to hurt you. I'm so sorry," Jace says. It seems like he means it.

I think for a moment before responding. There's nothing I can do to change what happened between us. Finally I reply, "I forgive you." I feel like a weight has been lifted as the words come out of my mouth.

"Thank you, that means so much to me." He looks over at me, but I don't return his gaze. I continue to stare out the front window. "So how can I make this up to you?" he asks.

I cross my arms over my chest, trying to remain calm. "We talked about being honest with each other so many times, and you never told me what you did. There is nothing you can do to make up for that. I can't trust you anymore."

"What if I get a divorce?" he pleads. "I've never been as happy with anyone the way I am when I'm with you. The risk of losing you made me realize how much I care about you. I really miss you."

"Jace, if you cared about me at all, you wouldn't have lied to me." I look him right in the eye.

His shoulders slump.

"Listen, I don't want to fight with you, and I don't want to get back together. Can we please just agree to be professional about this at work?"

He nods his head in agreement.

When we get to the hospital, Jace pulls into a parking spot.

"You don't have to stay."

"It's okay. I want to."

"Jace, please. I appreciate the ride, but I don't need you here," I say rudely.

He looks frustrated. "She might be your grandmother, but she is my friend, too. I want to stay for her," he snaps back.

I feel like a jerk now. I open my car door and walk ahead of him into the emergency room. The desk clerk won't let me back to see her right away because apparently they are running some tests.

I pace the waiting room. Worn-out magazines are scattered around the tables between the chairs. A young girl and her dad are sitting across the room while a vending machine hums in the other corner. I hate this waiting game. "Have you eaten dinner yet?" Jace asks.

I shake my head.

"Why don't we go down to the cafeteria and grab something to eat then?"

"I'm not hungry," I reply coldly.

"It's something to do while we wait."

I should eat something, since I missed lunch. "It's this way," I say as I start to head down the hallway. He follows. We don't say anything on the walk to the cafeteria, or even when we are in line to get food. When we reach the cash registers, Jace whips out his wallet to pay for mine before I even have the chance to dig for money in my purse. "Thanks," I mumble.

There is a decent-sized dinner crowd here. People of all ages and races are scattered throughout the room. I wonder what their stories are, why they are here. We sit down at the closest empty table. I pick up my chicken sandwich and take a bite.

Jace sighs. "I don't want things to be so awkward between us."

I finish chewing. "How exactly is it supposed to be between exes having dinner, when one of them is a lying married man?" I ask scornfully.

"If I could go back in time and change things, Abrielle, I would. I definitely wouldn't have rushed into marriage. I was just scared of being deported. I love America, and I love working at the shelter," he explains.

"Did you and Reagan ever date?" I ask, not that it matters anyway.

"No. She was the only female friend I had at the time. I think she always wanted it to be more, though." His response doesn't make me feel any better, but it does explain Reagan's behavior. "I hope you can understand how sorry I am." He looks contrite.

Honestly, I can't wrap my head around it. If he really felt that bad about lying, then he would have told me the truth sooner. "People make mistakes, Jace. You can't go back in time and change them, but you can learn from them." My mom always used to tell me that when I was younger. "I just hope that you are honest with the next girl in your life," I add.

He winces at that comment. His eyes look watery.

I check the time on my phone and change the subject. "It's been half an hour. Maybe they have an update on Grandma." We clear our trays and head back upstairs to the ER waiting room. "Any news on Faustina Peregrine?" I ask the desk clerk hopefully.

She types something into her computer. "Nothing yet."

"Thanks." I plop down on a faded chair. Jace sits down across from me, and we wait.

Chapter 27

I zip up the blue and white striped duffel bag that contains a few of Grandma's belongings.

"Ready?" Quin asks.

I look around. "Yeah, I think so." Grandma has already been in the hospital for one night. They want to keep her another night just to make sure she is okay. Her oncologist has decided to postpone treatment for a week, so that her body can recover while his team figures out a different treatment plan. Of course we waited almost all day for the doctor to tell us that, or I would have come over to the house sooner.

We head outside. It's dark and cloudy, and you can't see as many stars out tonight. Suddenly Reagan steps out of the shadows. Quin and I stop in our tracks. Luckily I have been able to avoid her so far at work. I really don't know what to say to her anyways.

"Reagan, hey—"

She cuts me off. "Do you know that all Jace talks about is how he can make things right with you and try to win you back? It's driving me crazy! He was supposed to fall in love with me, not you." She looks furious.

"I'm never getting back together with him, so there is nothing to worry about." I had no idea she felt that passionately about him. Or that he would talk to her about me. I thought I made it clear to him that we were over.

"Maybe if you're out of the picture completely, he will realize he had the perfect woman in front of him the whole time." She pulls out a gun and points it at me.

Without hesitation, Quin steps directly in front of me. We are about five feet away from Reagan—not close enough to get the gun out of her hands. "Put the gun down, Reagan, it will only make things worse," Quin says calmly.

"Get out of my way!" she yells.

Quin lunges toward her, but Reagan fires and he groans in pain, clutching his arm.

He has distracted her long enough for me to get closer. Instinctively, I do a front snap kick, and the gun goes sailing out of her hand. She looks at me, her face filled with rage. I find myself in parallel stance, waiting for her next move. It's been a while since I have done Taekwondo, but my muscles remember. Quin has managed to stand up. Blood drips down his left arm. Reagan takes off toward the gun, but I'm faster. I tackle her to the ground and pin her down on the grass. Quin rushes over as fast as he can with a pair of handcuffs from his truck. He hands them to me and I cuff her.

"What's Jace going to think of you now?" Quin asks her in contempt.

"He needs me, or he will get deported."

"Right, like he wants to stay married to a psychopath." Quin sneers. That just angers her more. Her body squirms underneath me as I hold her down. "As much as I hate saying this, because I don't want you to put yourself in danger," Quin comments, "You need to apply for the academy, Bri." I smile at him. I just might do that.

I can hear sirens around the corner, and the police finally arrive. Quin flashes his badge, and they take Reagan and press her into the back of the squad car. Paramedics rush over and attend to Quin's arm, wrapping a bandage around it to stop the bleeding. Luckily the bullet didn't hit a major artery.

Quin fills the cops in on what happened. As I watch him talk, I'm filled with gratitude. He took a bullet for me! I can't believe he actually lunged at someone pointing a gun. The paramedics interrupt my thoughts.

"We need to get you to a hospital right now," they tell Quin.

"Alright. Bri, can you take my truck?" He tosses me his keys.

* * * * *

I sit by Quin's bedside waiting for him to wake up. He looks so peaceful. His arm is wrapped up. It's been a few hours since his surgery. I keep replaying the scene in my mind. If he hadn't been there... It hurts me to think that he would risk his life for me, and know that we still can't be together. I love him so much. I don't think I ever stopped loving him. But I can't break my promise to my mom. I thought that living with Grandma would make it easier to forget about him, but being an hour away still wasn't far enough to get him out of my heart.

He opens his eyes and looks around. "Hey," he says quietly. His voice is hoarse. I run around to the other side of the bed and pour him a cup of water. "Thanks."

I move the bedside tray closer to him in case he needs anything. "How do you feel?"

He sits up a bit more in bed, then takes a sip. "My arm is a little sore."

"I wonder if the pain meds are wearing off."

"What time is it?"

"One a.m."

He looks at the bandage on his arm. "Good thing she shot this arm. I'd be pretty upset if she'd ruined my tattoo."

I smile. "That's what you're thinking about right now?" He shrugs his right shoulder.

"It had better leave a sweet scar," he adds.

I grab his hand and look into his eyes. "Quin, thank you," I say sincerely. He squeezes my hand and smiles. "A wise girl once told me that when you love someone, you make sacrifices for them." He pauses. I had said that to him the night we kissed. "I have been thinking a lot about the promise you made to your mom, and I think I can handle it. I can make that sacrifice if it means I get to be with you."

I smile. I don't know what to say.

"Soooo, what are you thinking?" he asks, doing a high school impression of me.

I laugh. I regularly asked him that in high school, always hoping his answer would be about me. Instead, he would make up random statements just to drive me crazy.

"I was thinking about how great a burrito would taste right now," I reply with a huge smile.

"Mmm, that does sound good," he says as he closes his eyes, imagining the taste.

"In all seriousness, though, I do want to be with you. I just need a little bit of time for some wounds to heal."

He nods his head. "I understand. Take as much time as you need."

"Thanks." I squeeze his hand, then let go.

He grabs the remote and turns the TV on, then glances at me. "Has it been long enough yet?" he asks, grinning.

I lean over and kiss his cheek. "I'm going to check on my grandma."

"Okay. Do you still have my truck keys?"

"Yeah," I reply as I reach into my pocket to pull them out.

"Good, 'cuz I would love some chips and salsa with that burrito."

I give him an *are you serious* look.

"C'mon—I took a bullet for you. I'm so hungry!"

"So, this is how it's going to be now?" I say trying to fight back a smile.

"Eh, maybe for a few weeks," he jokes.

Chapter 28

Quin sits next to me in my grandma's hospital room. He was released this morning. Grandma is sitting up in her bed. "How long has it been?" she asks.

"Half an hour."

"The nurse said he would be back in ten minutes. Why is this taking so long?"

I've never seen her this impatient before. "Are you hungry?" I ask.

"No, I just want to go home," she replies. Just then the doctor walks in. It's the boring one.

"Doctor Claussen, I thought I was going home an hour ago. Is everything okay?" Grandma asks.

He opens up a file folder, and says bluntly, "I'm afraid not," in his monotonous voice. Quin and I both stand up. "We ran a few scans, and it looks like the new chemo hasn't affected the tumors at all." I grab Grandma's hand. "The scans show that the tumors in your lungs have actually grown, some of them by two centimeters, and the cancer has spread to your spleen, and your pancreas."

I fight back tears. Quin grabs my other hand, and our fingers interlace. He squeezes.

Grandma looks confident. "Okay, so what does this mean?" she asks.

"Well, I would like to consult with a few other doctors and discuss some other treatment options."

"She's going to be okay, right?" I ask hopefully.

He closes his file folder. "We are going to do everything we can. I will call you as soon as we have a new treatment plan for you."

I look at Grandma for her response. She looks totally fine. I want to cry so badly, but I feel like if I do, she will think I have lost hope.

"Thank you, Doctor. Can I go home now?"

"Yes. Get some rest, and make the most of the day," he replies with a smile.

"I'm going to change out of this hospital gown," Grandma says when the doctor has left the room.

"Do you need any help?"

"No, I'm okay."

"Alright, we'll wait out in the hallway." I set her duffel bag on the bed, and Quin and I head out the door. I walk away from her room, so she can't hear me. "Ohh, I could just scream, then cry, then punch something. And then cry some more! This is so not fair!"

Quin scratches the back of his head. "I know, but the only thing you can do now is keep being there for her."

I look at him. He's right. "And the only thing I can do now is be here for you," he says as he wraps his arms around me. I lean into his chest, and he kisses my forehead. His embrace is soothing.

*****

"Do you want to get a second opinion?" I ask Grandma.

She shakes her head. "Doctor Claussen is the best in the nation. I trust him."

I sigh. Quin puts his hand on my leg, underneath the kitchen table. He had to drive us home, since I had no car at the hospital.

"How are you so calm right now?"

She stares at her half-eaten sandwich. "Because I have lived a full life. If I can't beat this, at least I will die knowing that I fought it the best I could."

I don't know how to respond. I feel like I have lost all hope, but I don't want her to know that. The doorbell rings.

"I'll get it." Quin stands up.

"I think it's very mature of you to continue working at the shelter after everything that has happened," Grandma says, changing the subject.

"I can't believe you had the guts to come here after everything!" we hear Quin yelling angrily.

I stand up from the table and run out into the hallway.

Jace is backing away from Quin on the front porch. "I just came over to apologize," he says.

"Quin!" I yell loudly from the hallway. He stops in his place, and I run up behind him.

Jace is standing there with his hands held up in surrender. "I just wanted to say 'I'm sorry' to both of you. I had no idea Reagan was going to act the way she did. She's going to be in jail for a while, and she's getting professional mental health treatment."

"Good. She needs it," Quin says disdainfully.

I put my hand on his arm, hoping it will calm him a bit.

"I would like to pay for your medical bills, Quin. I feel like this is all my fault," Jace offers. That's very generous of him.

But Quin refuses. "I don't need your help."

"Can I have a word with Jace?" Grandma asks from the doorway.

I wonder how long she has been standing there. Quin and I go back in the house, and I push the door so that it's almost closed. I leave a sliver of space open to listen. We stand behind it intently.

"Jace, I'm really disappointed about this whole situation," Grandma starts.

"I'm really sorry."

"Did Abrielle decide to forgive you?"

"Yeah."

"Good, then I forgive you, too, for hurting her... I hope you learned from your mistakes. Jace, the doctor didn't actually say it, but I'm dying. If I could tell you only one more thing, it would be to forgive others, and not to dwell on the mistakes you have made. Instead, learn from them and move forward."

Jace doesn't say anything.

"I think it would be best if you give Abrielle some space. I'm sure that will be hard since you are working together, but she needs time to heal."

"I understand. Thank you."

I can hear Jace's footsteps as he walks down the porch steps. Quin pulls me away from the door. Grandma walks in and shuts the door behind her, then looks at us. "I know you were listening. That advice was for you, too. Don't keep making the same mistake that you have made for years, of not acting on your feelings for each other."

Quin and I look at each other. She points her finger at Quin. "You'd better take care of her when I'm gone." Quin nods his head. I hate the way she is talking, as if she knows she won't be around much longer. "Can you make me a green juice please?" she asks me as she walks toward her bedroom.

"Yes," I reply as I glance at Quin, hoping he will say something to make sense of all this. Instead he follows me into the kitchen to help. I throw some vegetables into the juicer with some ice.

"I hate to leave, but I have to work tonight," he says as he hands me a cup for the juice.

"Okay, thanks for everything," I say as I lean in to hug him.

"I'll call you tomorrow." I nod my head. I don't want him to let go. It's been a really long day.

Grandma is sitting in the rocking chair in her room. I set the juice down on the nightstand next to her, then sit on the edge of her bed.

"Hopefully the doctors will call us tomorrow with a better treatment plan."

She sighs. "I'm in a lot of pain, Abrielle."

"I'll get your medicine," I say as I stand up.

"No. Sit. The medicine isn't helping."

I slowly sit back down on her bed. "The doctors are going to figure something out," I offer.

"Abrielle," she says gently. "The sooner you accept that I cannot beat this, the easier it will be for you when I'm gone."

"You're giving up?" I ask dejectedly.

"I'm going to make the most of each day that I have left. Spending all day in bed and throwing up all the time? That's no way to spend the time I still have. The chemo is too hard to handle, and the cancer is too advanced for it to work."

I start to cry. I can't help it. She slowly rises from the chair and then sits down next to me on the bed. "I get to see my husband soon. Do you know how long I have waited for that?" she asks as she wraps her arm around me. I wipe a tear away and look at her.

"You're not scared to die?"

"No. I'm at peace with dying," she replies calmly.

"I'm not."

"We will be together again someday." She takes my hand. I'm supposed to be the one consoling her, and yet throughout this whole journey she has been the one consoling me.

Chapter 29

I stare at the security footage. People are milling around in the sleeping dorms, getting their cots ready for the night. Lights Out is in a few minutes. I don't know if I can keep working here. Dalilah has cut my shifts back as I requested, so I rarely see Jace now, but it still feels awkward. I still have to walk past his desk multiple times a night—and Reagan's old desk, too. Cameron took over for her. How am I supposed to forget about them when we all work together?

"So, we're still friends, right?" Isaac asks as he stands across from my workstation.

"Yeah, why wouldn't we be?" I ask as I spin to face him.

He plops down in his desk chair. "I just thought you might hate me, since Jace is my best friend." He scoots his chair over to mine.

"Nothing that happened is your fault."

"I know, but I knew he was married and didn't tell you." He looks down at his hands.

"What was going on between you and Reagan?" I ask.

He shrugs his shoulders. "I think she was just using me to make Jace jealous." There is sadness in his voice.

"Wait, did you really like her?" I ask in surprise.

"Yeah...until she went all berserk on you."

I smile. "Well, before she tried to kill me, she made a comment about how Jace had the perfect girl right in front of him the whole time. I think *she* had the perfect guy in front of her the whole time and just didn't know it," I say sincerely.

"Thanks," he says with a smile. He sighs. "Oh man, life sucks sometimes, huh?" If he only knew half the things I've been through.

"Yeah, but we can sit here and wallow in self-pity, or we can accept the fact that what happened is not what we had hoped, and deal with it. Move on. Focus on the things that *are* going our way."

He nods and smiles, then sighs. "I hate to ruin this Hallmark moment, but one of us needs to go turn the lights out in the dorms."

I smirk. "All I heard you say just now was that you were going to go turn the lights out."

He snickers and heads toward the dorms.

I pull up my e-mail account and begin to draft a letter of resignation. It's hard to find the words. I have worked here since I was sixteen. But school starts next week, and I want to be there as much as I can for Grandma. Dalilah will understand.

*****

I pace back and forth in the living room as Grandma speaks to Dr. Claussen on the phone. I can't believe he has made us wait three days to hear back. Three days! That's an eternity when you are a cancer patient waiting to find out about a treatment plan or test results. "That won't work. But I can come in tomorrow." I stare at her quietly. "I understand. I will be there tomorrow afternoon... Thank you... Good-bye."

She hangs up the phone and looks at me. "I qualify for a clinical study that will start tomorrow," she states calmly.

I am not sure if I should be excited or worried about that.

"That's good news, right?" A clinical study sounds like it could either go terribly wrong or terrifically well.

She shrugs her shoulders. "I will have to stay at the hospital for three weeks. They'll need to monitor my body's response to the treatment. There are a lot of risks. Either way, I will probably end up in the hospital longer."

I sit down next to her. "You're not going in until tomorrow, though, right?"

She nods her head.

"Let's do something fun today, then!" I want to help keep her mind off the fact that she will be confined for three long weeks.

"I know it's a weekday, but let's have a big cookout. Invite everyone," she suggests excitedly, as if she already had this planned. I'm not sure how many people will be able to come on such short notice. I don't want her to be disappointed.

"Are you sure that's what you want to do today?"

"Yes. Let's go to lunch, then we can pick up a few things for dinner. It's still early, so I'll call everyone now to invite them," she insists.

She calls a few of her neighbors, while I call Dad, Ariana, Quin, and Jocelyn. We go to her favorite restaurant for lunch. After we eat, I insist on dropping her off at home to rest while I shop for the food for dinner tonight.

*****

Dad and Ariana walk into the kitchen with a bag of decorations for the party. "Grandma is still sleeping," I say.

"Good, because I know she would object to streamers and balloons. But I want this to be special since she is going to be in the hospital for a while." She decorates the porch while Dad and I start cooking.

"Who is coming tonight?" he asks. We don't have any family members who live in town.

"I really don't know," I reply.

I can hear Grandma moving around in her room, so I go to check on her. She is already wearing her favorite party dress. There are a few bruises on her legs that I hadn't noticed before.

"Which scarf?" she asks, holding up the gray one and the blue one.

"Gray," I reply as walk over to her. She sits down, and I arrange it on her head. "You look beautiful, Grandma," I say sincerely.

"Thank you."

I pull out my phone to take a picture of us. "Smile!"

The doorbell rings. "It's six o'clock already?" she asks.

I can hear Jocelyn and Quin talking to Ariana in the living room. I help Grandma walk out to meet them. Jocelyn has a big gift box in her hand.

"Hey!" she exclaims when she sees us. "You look fantastic, Ms. P!" she says as she throws her free arm around Grandma in a hug.

"Thank you. Let's all go outside," she suggests.

The doorbell rings again. Quin and Jocelyn go outside with Grandma while I answer the door. It's Dalilah Pierce. I am surprised to see her.

"Hi, Abrielle," she says courteously.

"Hi," I say. She holds out a greeting card. "I hope you don't mind, but when your grandma told me she was starting a clinical study soon, I suggested that the neighbors bring a card or gift over to lift her spirits."

"I think that's a great idea," I say with gratitude. I wish I had thought of that. "Everyone is out on the porch. This way," I add, leading her outside.

After about an hour, the deck is filled with neighbors and Grandma's friends. I stand against the deck railing by Quin, watching her talk to all her guests. There is a sparkle in her that I haven't seen in a while. Quin puts his arm around my waist. "Stop thinking about what it will be like when she's gone, and just live in the moments that you have left with her," he says softly. I lean in to his shoulder. He knows me too well.

*****

Two years later

The deliveryman hands me a beautiful arrangement of red roses. I set them down on the counter and open the card:

> *I can't wait to call you my wife later on today.*
> *Love,*
> *Your Soon-to-Be-Husband*
> *P.S. I'm glad we waited...*

I smile as I tuck the card back in the envelope. Jocelyn, Ariana, and Natalia rush over to me in their jade bridesmaid's dresses to smell the bouquet. "Ready?" Jocelyn asks me.

"Yes!" I reply with the biggest smile. She hands me the bouquet of blue forget-me-nots. Dad walks over and links his arm with mine. "Your mom would be so proud of you," he says gently.

"And so would Grandma," Ariana adds. The music begins, and the girls start walking down the aisle with the groomsmen. I smile at Dad. The music fades, and I can hear people standing up inside the church. I take a deep breath as the opening strains of my processional music begin. Dad walks me around the corner, and we start down the aisle. Family, friends, and colleagues from the police academy fill the pews. They are all staring at me. I should make eye contact with them and smile, but I can't take my eyes off of him. I have dreamt of this day for so long.

Excitement surges through my body. *This is really happening!* Finally we get to the end of the aisle, and Dad shakes Quin's hand, then hugs me and takes his seat.

"You look gorgeous," Quin whispers in my ear as he takes my hand. He gazes into my eyes, and my heart melts. Together, we walk toward the priest, ready to begin this thrilling new *adventure* in our lives.